FEB 2 7 2006

FEB 2 7 2006

FEB 2 7 2006

FEB 2 7 2006

FEB 2 7 2006

P9-BJA-574

Ghoul Reporter Digs Up Zombies!

Created by
LINDA ELLERBEE

AVON BOOKS NEW YORK

A Division of HarperCollinsPublishers

My deepest thanks to Katherine Drew, Anne-Marie Cunniffe, Lori Seidner, Whitney Malone, Roz Noonan, Alix Reid and Susan Katz, without whom this series of books would not exist. I also want to thank Christopher Hart, whose book, *Drawing on the Funny Side of the Brain*, retaught me how to cartoon. At age 11, I was better at it than I am now. Honest.

Drawings by Linda Ellerbee

Avon Books® is a registered trademark
of HarperCollins Publishers Inc.

Ghoul Reporter Digs Up Zombies!
Copyright © 2000 by Lucky Duck Productions, Inc.
Produced by By George Productions, Inc.

Library of Congress Cataloging-in-Publication Data
Ellerbee, Linda.
    Ghoul reporter digs up zombies! / created by Linda Ellerbee.
        p.   cm. — (Get real ; #5)
    Summary: Sixth-grade school journalist Casey Smith investigates the apparent haunting of a local cemetery.
    ISBN 0-06-440759-4 (pbk.) — ISBN 0-06-028249-5 (lib. bdg.)
    [1. Ghosts—Fiction.   2. Journalism—Fiction.   3. Schools—Fiction.]
I. Title
PZ7.E42845 Gf   2000   00-23960
[Fic]—dc21   CIP
                                                                    AC

Typography by Carla Weise
1   2   3   4   5   6   7   8   9   10
❖
First Edition

For the kids,
who always get real

Ghouls Infest New England Town!

MY NAME IS Casey Smith, and I am living in a bad dream.

Just look at my street.

Tombstones were on every front lawn. Giant webs with black spiders in them were on every front porch. And then there was my weird neighbor, who talks to her cats. She had two ghoul-faced zombies sitting on her patio furniture. Were they having zombie tea and a zombie chat? Possibly the topic was skin care, since their faces were rotting off their skulls.

Halloween weirdness was definitely here. Every house was a haunted house. I already thought my dinky town, Abbington, was totally dead. But this was ridiculous.

Don't get me wrong. I love Halloween. What a

1

bummer that I'm too old to justify a night of trick-or-treating. I guess you've got to turn eleven and go to middle school and start acting old at some point. But I was going to miss traipsing through Creepsville after dark. All that free chocolate, just for wearing a costume made to look bloody with splats of ketchup. It had always been one night of the year when the town felt different. Spooky different.

That is, if you can feel spooky covered in French-fry dipping sauce.

But Halloween hadn't arrived yet. It was more than a week away. And today was Thursday. That meant two whole days until the weekend. Two whole days of school. In fact, I was on my way to school, feeling sort of bored with everything. So I hunkered down on my bike and imagined that girl-eating ghouls were chasing me down the street. I pedaled faster on my bike, a metallic blue Illusion 2000 with eight gears, mud tires and a flat-repair kit strapped under the seat. A girl's got to be able to fix her own tire in an emergency.

I reached up to scratch under my helmet, which always plasters my hair against my head. Not that it really mattered. I've resigned myself to the fact that I have boring brown hair. Boring brown eyes. Boring brown freckles whenever I get caught in the sun. Is it any wonder that I was

2

spending my morning pretending to be a monster snack?

I sped around a corner, jumping the curb the way I'd seen this extreme biker do on TV. It helped wake me up.

At seven A.M., I felt a little undead myself.

Then I saw one of the living walking down the street ahead of me.

"Ringo?" I called out as I got closer. No mistake. Only my bud Ringo wears purple socks and Birkenstocks. It's his trademark. It sort of warns anyone who doesn't know him that you're about to meet a guy who stood in a different line when they were handing out normal brains.

"Hey, Casey!" he said, turning to watch my killer skid-stop. "You could write your name in the street doing that."

I couldn't take my eyes off his hair. It was purple. Like pass-me-the-purple-crayon purple. "Or I could write messages to aliens," I said, raising an eyebrow. "Aliens from Planet Purple Hair."

Ringo touched his hair as if he hadn't looked in the mirror this morning. Usually it's an unremarkable brown. At least his eyes were still gray. And the Ringo grin was still intact. "You like it? I was trying it out for my costume."

"That depends," I said. "Are you going for Barney—or a human eggplant?"

Ringo tilted his head. "What came first, the chicken or the eggplant?"

"Ringo—purple hair? Explain," I ordered. You have to keep Ringo focused. Otherwise, he'll go off on a riff about anything from toe jam to cheerleading moves.

He stopped at a cluster of pumpkins huddled on the stone fence of one house and lifted the lid off a jack-o'-lantern. "No candle in this one. Guess it's just a jack-o. Minus the lantern."

I urged him on, and he replaced the pumpkin lid. "Ringo—your hair?"

"Melody said it was supposed to wash out," he said.

Melody is from England. She moved here in the middle of the semester. She and Ringo have this artist thing going.

"I think you'll have to wash your head in industrial-strength acid to get that out," I said, spotting the bike racks in front of the school. "Come with me to lock this baby up."

After we secured my bike, we headed to the *Real News* office for a before-school meeting. *Real News* is Trumbull Middle School's newspaper, which is a newly restarted thing as of this year. A few years ago, the students just stopped publishing it. Did they lose their minds or what?

See, I have a nose for news. Really. My nose

actually tingles when I get near a story. But more on that later. Last month, I decided to put *Real News* back in circulation. And I did, with some help from a few other sixth graders. Like my friend Ringo, who draws a weekly cartoon about a dude named Simon.

"Why do you even need a costume, anyway?" I asked as we cruised toward the storage room that we use as our office. "Kids our age don't go trick-or-treating."

"The Trumbull Halloween party that Megan is organizing," Ringo reminded me. "It's a yearbook fund-raiser."

I let out a moan. The party was all our *Real News* editor-in-chief, Megan O'Connor, had talked about for days. Of course, she was the key organizer. She's the key organizer to everything yippy skippy at school.

"And the thing is, there's a prize for best costume," Ringo went on. "I love prizes. Did you ever eat through a box of cereal just to get the dumb plastic toy inside?"

Did I mention that Ringo loses focus? "What's the big prize?" I asked.

Ringo's eyes lit up. "Winner gets a free yearbook."

"Whoopee!" I yelled. "How could I forget something as amazing as that?"

I could picture Megan dressed like the good witch of Trumbull Middle School. Or the fairy princess of the popular people. Whatever her costume, it would definitely be sweet and fluffy and covered in glitter. I knew that much.

I was still thinking about the Princess of Pink's party when I heard a strange sound come from the newsroom.

What was that? Ringo and I stepped inside and stopped dead in our tracks. The room was dark. Someone had pulled the curtains over the grimy grated windows.

There was another moan and a muffled noise from the back of the room. I flinched and took a step back, bumping into Ringo. He gripped my arm.

"Oh my gosh, Ringo! Look out!"

Skeletons Discovered in Newsroom Closets!

WE DUCKED, BUT it was too late. A full-sized skeleton was coming at us fast. Before I could escape, it slammed into me. Hard.

"Ringo, help! HELP!" My arms flailed wildly.

Ringo grabbed the skeleton and yanked it off me. For a minute I thought he was going to karate-chop the thing into firewood, but something was tangled around him.

"What the . . . ?" he said, checking it out. "Casey, there's a string."

Then we heard the laughter. The lights flicked on. So did my temper.

I spun around and saw the dirty culprits: Tyler and Gary. Gary manned the light switch. Tyler stood behind the full-sized skeleton, which hung from a little wheeled cart. And they were still

7

laughing their booties off.

My blood got warm. Then hot. Then it straight-up boiled.

"You guys!" I yelled, rubbing my arms. "Watch carefully and you'll see the knuckle bone connect to the face bone."

"Casey, wait!" Gary said, holding up a hand. "Don't attack me! It was Tyler's idea. He talked Ms. Branston into loaning him Mr. Bones, the science department's new skeleton."

I glared at Tyler. Tyler McKenzie has brown hair and a crooked grin that knocks my scales off whenever I get crusty. He's also the cutest boy in school. To me, anyway. And I think I'm up there on his list, too. But in Boyland that translates into playing jokes on me and punching me in the arm for no reason.

And Gary? He's got short black hair and skin the color of hot chocolate. Lots of girls think Gary Williams is the cutest boy in school. They used to "ooh" and "ahh" over his baby dreads, which he recently cut off to make his football helmet fit better. He's totally devoted to all things jock, which makes him a fine sportswriter. Gary is one of the few African-American guys at Trumbull. He's quick to point out that he's the only black kid in this class or that one. Or how he stood out in the Abbington summer baseball league because he was the only black all-star. Gary is black and proud of it.

I dropped my backpack onto the lime-green and black polka-dotted table that Ringo named Dalmatian Station. The table, which Megan got from her grandmother, is hideous. It's grown on me, but it's still a sign of how we are unappreciated by the school. Besides the dotted table, we did have computers, but also a bunch of ratty old desks, sagging chairs and clunky file cabinets.

"That really spiked my adrenaline," Ringo said, straddling a chair beside me. He flipped open his red spiral notebook and started drawing.

"Right. Nothing like a good skeleton slam to get the day started."

"Seriously, Casey," Gary said, dropping into a chair. "It was just a joke. Nothing to wig about. Just calm down."

"I'll have you know it really hurt having Mr. Fatty barrel into me," I said, hands on both my hips like an angry mother. Not to mention that two boys were laughing at me. At my expense.

Calm down? I don't think so.

Tyler looked concerned. "Are you hurt or something? Are you mad?"

I could tell I had him squirming, but before I could take advantage—

"Oh please!" Gary jumped in. "She's not hurt.

Casey just can't stand being the victim of a prank."

"Don't you have anything better to do, Gary?" I asked. "Like work on the paper? The reason we all tolerate each other?"

"Um, Casey?" Ringo blinked at me. "Remember? We wrapped this week's edition early. Yesterday."

He was right. We'd even gotten early approval from our advisor, Mr. Baxter, who is always running late and running out the door. Not that it makes him a bad guy. He's a cool English teacher and a hands-off advisor. Works for me.

Ringo went on. "There's nothing to do today except talk about—"

But before he could finish, Megan rushed in, lugging a fat phonebook.

"Guys! Party-planning emergency!" Her entrance was so dramatic, I thought that any minute she was going to hold the back of her hand to her forehead and fake fainting. "Ms. Nachman promised the gym to the chess club for a tournament Halloween weekend! Now I have to find a place for the party—in less than a week!"

The horror! What *would* she do?

Megan opened the phonebook and let her pink enameled fingernails do the walking. Without another word, she began to make a list of places to call. The bowling alley, the lodge at the lake, the catering hall in the Abbington Motel with the tacky fountains in the lobby. . .

"Whoa." Toni whipped into the doorway and paused. "This place is dark as a tomb," she said. Toni Velez is our staff photographer and resident Girl With Attitude. You'll see what I mean. She went straight to the windows and yanked open the flowered curtains. Megan had made them out of some bedsheets her mom was tossing out.

Toni had started to set her backpack down when she spotted the skeleton. Her bracelets jangled as she crossed herself. "What's that doing in here?" she asked.

"My mistake," Tyler said, glancing uncomfortably at me. "And since it's not scoring points with anyone, why don't I just get it out of here."

Toni stepped back as Tyler wheeled Mr. Bones past her. She couldn't take her eyes off the skeleton. Tugging on her red-streaked curls, she watched nervously until Tyler had moved the rattling old ghoul into the hall.

"Toni, Halloween is just a commercial holiday promoted by the candy industry," I said, trying to calm her down a little. "It's possible that the dental industry is in on it, too."

"Save the save-the-world speech," she said. See what I mean? Major 'tude. "Halloween is not what scares me, Casey. In Mexico, they respect the dead . . . and their bones. And their spirits." She crossed herself again.

"Is it a Catholic thing?" Gary asked.

"It is what it is," Toni snapped. "And it's coming soon—the Day of the Dead. I am just not into making fun of dead people."

Ringo snapped his fingers. "I've heard of that. Everyone celebrates the lives of people who lived before us. People decorate graves and stay up all night to welcome back the spirits of those who've died. When is it?"

"November first and second," Toni answered, digging through her pack.

"Cool," Gary added as Tyler popped back in. "I love those stories about dead people who come back."

"Yeah," Tyler added. "Zombies and ghosts. The undead."

Sitting at a desk, I logged on to a computer. "You guys are suckers for urban legends."

"There's got to be some truth to the stories about haunted things," Gary insisted. "Otherwise, people wouldn't keep repeating them."

"Hello?" I reached over, pretending to knock

12

on Gary's head. "Is that how you confirm a story? By the number of people who yap about it?"

"Okay, maybe some of it's made up," Tyler jumped in. "But there's one place in Abbington that's definitely haunted."

Gary's eyebrows rose. "Purser Farms," he said, as if he was saying "You have one week to live."

Tyler nodded solemnly. Toni hugged herself, shivering. Megan, who was off on that party-planning astral plane, muttered something about enough room for a hayride.

Purser Farms is this folksy nature-hike area that has a creek, a pond and acres of hills. It also has a small cemetery stretching over the hillside. The cemetery was started by the Purser family. They don't bury people there anymore, so it sort of looks like a park with marble statues. I'd gone hiking around there a bunch of times and had never walked into the walking dead.

"Purser Farms?" I scoffed. "No way."

"I have the four-one-one. That place is creeped," Gary said. "My brother, Brandon, saw something in the cemetery a few years back. A body floating over a grave."

"Yeah," Tyler said, "and lots of people have heard weird sounds there—moaning and scraping.

Like zombies are trying to scratch their way out of their graves."

"You guys are hopeless. I am out of this conversation." I sat down, pulled the keyboard onto my lap and propped my feet on the desk.

I'm not big on fashion. Anything beyond jeans and sweatshirt is out on a limb for me. Except for my Converse sneakers. Last I checked, I had eight pairs in eight different colors.

I looked over at Toni, who was sitting at Dalmatian Station. She had put her headphones on to drown out the zombie talk. Megan was still compiling her list. Her brows were knit. The toe of her petite loafer tap-tapped nervously on the floor. In sunny, temperate Meganland, these are signs of a storm blowing in.

"There's some legend about the statues in the cemetery," Gary continued, turning his baseball cap around so that the bill was in back. "That they follow people around."

"Awesome!" Ringo looked up from his notebook and smiled. "Like a wax museum."

"Yeah, if the stuff at a wax museum moved," Tyler pointed out.

I tried to get online so that I could e-mail my friend Griffin. Griffin was my best Abbington friend until he moved a gazillion miles away to Baltimore. But I kept getting a busy signal. I was still ignoring Gary and Tyler. Lot of good that did.

"But what about the best Purser scare story?" Gary asked.

Toni yanked off her headset. "How 'bout you guys exit? Go talk about candy-corn encounters somewhere else."

But Gary was on a roll. "Here's what I heard." He spoke quietly, as if he was talking over a campfire. "These two kids were waiting out a storm in their car near the Purser property. They heard a knock on the car door, but all they saw was rain pouring down the window. There was another knock. Then another. Then a flash of lightning, and they saw it: There was a bloody, rotting zombie outside, yanking on the handle and pounding on the door. That zombie wanted in."

"Yeah!" Tyler gave Gary a high five. "I've heard this story, too."

"The teenagers were so freaked, they started the car and drove off through the storm. And they got away. Only when they parked at home and got out, they noticed it. A hand was clutching the door handle of their car!"

Toni pressed her fingers against her forehead. "Did I ask you to chill or what? What part didn't you hear?"

"What is it about boys and body parts?"

Megan murmured absently as she flipped a page in the phonebook.

"Are you sure it wasn't a hook?" I asked, unable to believe that these nitwit boys could believe such an obvious urban legend.

"A hook?" Ringo asked.

I looked over at the cartoon he was drawing.

"Listen guys," I said, canceling my sign-on, "you're just falling for old stories that get passed down from older kids to younger kids over and over again. Get a grip."

"How do you know they're not true?" Tyler asked, putting a hand on my shoulder.

That would be Tyler's hand. On my shoulder. Did you get that?

I was ready to go into a major debate with Tyler when it hit me. I wasn't going to prove anything to these chill-seeking boys. But I could prove that the Purser land wasn't haunted. My nose started to tingle.

"That's it!" I jerked up in my chair and accidentally knocked his hand off my shoulder. I have this habit of clunking into Tyler all the time. It's a wonder that he comes near me, considering the bruises.

"That's not a bad idea at all," I continued. "A story on Purser Cemetery. The legends. The lies. And the lunatic kids who believe in them."

Megan paused, pink pen poised in the air. "A story for *Real News*?" Her editorial instinct is always on. "That sounds awfully . . . awful."

That's Megan's approach to news. She wants to spoon-feed kids sugary pieces about comfy things like winning teams and yearbook parties. I prefer stories with some meat. Something you need a fork and knife to really dig into.

"I have to admit, I'm into it," Gary said. "It's timely."

"Yeah," Ringo said, pulling a package of cookies out of his backpack. "And Casey's just the one to prove that ghosts are no Fig Newton of the imagination."

But Megan was shaking her head. "I don't think so—"

"I'm not pitching it yet," I said. "Give me time to work it up."

Megan's mouth puckered in disagreement.

But she went back to her list.

And I went back to planning my next front-page story. I could see the headline now:

GIRL REPORTER DIGS UP ZOMBIES, UNCOVERS A LOT OF HOT AIR!

CHAPTER 3

Ghosts—Real Phenomena, or Fig Newtons of the Imagination?

THE REST OF the day was whatever.

As I biked home, past all the ghoulish décor on everyone's lawns and porches, I kept thinking about the Purser property and the legends about it. When I got home I went straight upstairs to my room to e-mail Griffin.

I was halfway through an e-mail explaining how suckered the boys were by the zombie stories when I realized something. Griffin was in Europe with his parents this week.

I deleted the e-mail and took off my Converse sneakers. Green today.

Stretching out my legs, I wiggled my toes inside my socks. These feet were made for traveling. I stared at my sneakers for a minute. I turned one over and picked at a little rock stuck in a rubber groove in the sole. Then I suddenly chucked the thing across my room at my closet. Direct hit.

I never go anywhere.

I wished I were in Europe, too. Looking at art. Trying to decode strange languages. Eating pizza in Italy, buttery croissants in France. Travel is so key for a writer. And I'm stuck here in Abbington.

Sometimes I think I should have gone to Southeast Asia with my parents. They are a part of this program called Doctors Without Borders. It takes doctors all over the world to help people deal with disasters like hurricanes or nuclear spills. My older brother got to go along, mostly because my parents wanted to keep close watch on him. He's a teenager, and last year his grades suffered. Suffered from a bad case of Don't Feel Like Studying.

I got to stay here in a tiny town at the base of the Berkshires (taller than hills but shorter than mountains). A place where the kids are so bored, they believe wild stories about bodies floating above graves.

Get real.

But even if Abbington was the land of the undead, home was heaven. My parents had left me under the care of the top journalist in the world.

She also happens to be my gram. My grandmother was a hotshot journalist in Washington,

D.C., and New York and dozens of other places around the world. Now she keeps an eye on me and is working on a book about her life. What's not to like? I decided a long time ago that I was going to follow in her footsteps.

Even if I do it in hightop sneakers.

My computer screen hummed, calling me back. Time to get something done. Like work on my antizombie story for *Real News*. Even if my story wouldn't land any organized criminals behind bars or save an endangered species, it was still better than writing about the yearbook fund-raiser.

I logged on to the Internet and started a search for strange-but-true stories. There were a lot. Apparently poltergeists and supernatural occurrences were no strangers to Internet browsers.

As my room grew dark, I sifted through creepy stuff about ghosts haunting houses, old hotels and restaurants. There was even a haunted toy store. Little kids had dropped toys and run off crying. Employees refused to stock the shelves at night. Who was this ghost, the anti-Santa?

Some of the stories were edgier than others. There was this one story about an old farmhouse that was supposed to be haunted by the people who built it. It was a long house, with the family room and kitchen on one end, an entry hall in the middle and the bedrooms on the other end. Both ends were carpeted, but the entry hall had a stone-tiled floor. The people who lived there said that every night they could hear footsteps padding across the floor of the family room, plunking on the tiles, then padding along the carpet of the hallway outside the bedroom. Then they heard a bedroom door open and close.

A psychic came and told them that they were actually hearing the original owners walk through the house to go to bed every night. Creepy.

I was sitting there in the dark, looking at my screen, getting into these hard-to-not-believe tales, when I felt a hand on my shoulder.

"Aaaahhh!" I screamed.

"Waaaahhhh!" the hand screamed back. I spun around in my chair as the light went on.

"Casey!" Gram clutched her jacket closer. "I was concerned when I pulled up and the house was dark. You scared the stuffing out of me."

"Gram, jeez!" I said. "I thought you were a zombie or something."

"A zombie?" Her face scrunched up. "I may be a grandmother, but I'm not that old. And since when do zombies march in with Chinese food?"

"You're not old, Gram. You're seasoned," I said. Then I told her about my new assignment at Purser Cemetery.

She kissed me on the head. "Come, eat, we'll talk. I've got stories."

"Ghost stories?" I asked, following her downstairs to the kitchen.

"I prefer to call them supernatural occurrences," she said as we sat down. "But yes, I've come across a few unexplained sightings."

I opened a carton of rice and watched the steam curl like a wispy ghost. Nothing like a belly full of hot-and-sour shrimp and a head full of ghost stories to give a girl bad dreams.

The next day, I was sitting in social studies staring at the blackboard like a zombie myself. Sometimes school is so boring, I feel like I could move pencils with my mind.

Then Ms. Hinkel said something that snapped me out of my trance. "For the next week, we're going to combine social studies classes for a special unit on global studies," she said with so much enthusiasm you'd think she was offering us free ice cream. "You'll work in pairs, and you'll research how people in Mexico celebrate a holiday that occurs at this time of year. They call it the Day of the Dead."

I immediately thought of Toni. I looked over at her chair, but she wasn't in it. Where was that curly-haired shower of attitude?

"Working with a partner, you will practice and write about some of the customs from the holiday," Ms. Hinkel said. She explained that we could cook some type of traditional food or go to the graveyard and clean off ancestors' graves to make the spirits happy. She added that if we didn't have any ancestors buried in Abbington, we could "adopt" some.

I knew right away I'd be one of the kids cleaning graves. Gram's idea of cooking is ordering a good combo plate over the phone. She blames it on living in New York City.

I opened my notebook and started taking notes:

DAY OF THE DEAD

1. Cook traditional foods (I don't think so)

2. Clean grave. Adopt ancestor.

E-Z.

In addition, each student had to make a family tree of one person buried in Purser Cemetery. "It's an interesting cemetery," Ms. Hinkel went on, "quite historic. The three hundred or so people buried there are the founders of Abbington. Also, you'll see that it's divided into two sections. Can anyone tell me why?"

Jessica Rundel waved her hand in the air until Ms. Hinkel nodded at her. "Because they wanted a separate section for the rich people?"

"Actually, it's divided along racial lines," Ms. Hinkel explained. "The graveyard was set up in the early eighteen hundreds, when people didn't bury black people and white people next to each other."

People were so strange in the olden days.

As I finished writing the assignment, I realized kids were already pairing off. Tyler and Ringo had joined forces. So had Gary and Megan. Why didn't anyone ask me? I may be the last kid picked for dodgeball, but this was ridiculous.

Suddenly Ms. Hinkel asked me who I was paired with, and I got a little nervous. I didn't want to look like a major loner. Then I remembered that Toni knew all about the Day of the Dead.

"My partner is Toni Velez," I said, like it was an obvious fact. With Toni as a partner, this project was going to be a piece of cake. Or candy corn, as the case may be.

I couldn't wait to tell Toni, which was easier thought than done. She never showed up for social studies, but Ms. Hinkel didn't seem fazed.

Had Toni gone home sick? After class I swung by her locker and by the newsroom—no luck.

Finally, after the last bell, I bolted to her locker and planted myself there.

"Hey girl, you lost?" Toni smacked her gum as she sauntered up to her locker.

"Toni—hey," I said, standing up. "No, I'm just waiting for you. We're partners in social studies."

No response. Toni flipped through the combo on her locker and started digging through her stuff.

"It might be fun, Toni," I said, as if I was talking about a pizza party. "We have to clean graves and get to know a dead person. Real bonding stuff."

"I don't dig graveyards, girl," Toni said without even looking at me. Then she zipped up her backpack and walked away.

"Hey, wait up, Toni. Jeez," I said, padding after her like a dog. "Listen, you can—"

"Don't tell me to listen," she interrupted, stopping dead in her tracks. Then she pointed an orange-polished nail in my face. "Don't tell me what to do. Ever! Got that?"

Obviously something was wrong. Way wrong.

But I wasn't about to ask her. I pictured her biting my head off, chewing it like bubble gum, then spitting it out on the sidewalk with all the other splats of gum. The thing is, you don't ever want to be on Toni's bad side. Get on her bad list and you'll wish you were living in Idaho.

"Okay, okay, sorry," I muttered. "I just wanted to tell you we can get two assignments done at once. You can take the photos of the graveyard for my *Real News* story when we go to clean graves for Ms. Hinkel. In fact, we can go there right now and get it over with. That's all."

She looked down at her platform shoes, short flowered skirt and bright blue top. "I am not ruining my clothes in a graveyard."

"Well, you could go home and change. I'll meet you here in, like, forty minutes?" I could tell she was softening. After all, my head was still on my shoulders.

"Whatever. Fine."

Then Toni was out the school's front door and down the steps faster than you can say "Wicked Witch of the West."

Zombie Gophers Haunt Deadwood Cemetery!

TONI WAS LATE.

I practiced jumping the curbs on my bike. I practiced my skid-stops. I even tried writing my name with skids in the street. Don't ask me how it came out looking more like CAZEY. Anyone reading fast was going to think it said CRAZY.

Which wasn't far from the truth. I'd waited for cranky Toni for half an hour, and I was itching to get to that graveyard. Finally Toni rolled up on her bike.

"Where have you been?" I asked, trying not to sound too peeved.

"Nunyuh." She adjusted the chin strap of her helmet.

"What's 'nunyuh'?" I asked, feeling annoyed through and through now.

"None-yuh business, get it?" she said, like I was hard of hearing. "Let's roll."

Toni rode fast. I had to work the gears of my Illusion 2000 to keep pace with her. She cut across lawns, turned down alleys, took shortcuts I never knew about. Then we turned down the long straight road that leads to Purser. The wind seemed to whisper, "Gooooo baaaackkk. . . ." But I chalked it up to my imagination. I could smell the birch-tree bark. The leaves and twigs on the rocky dirt road snapped and crackled under our wheels.

It was a dark road because supertall old birch trees shaded the whole area. The trees had leafy branches that swayed and waved in the wind like long hair. Like the hair of supertall ghosts. Ghosts who lined up along the road, leading the way to Purser.

I had never noticed them before. The way they seemed to lure you to Purser, like you were never coming back.

NOTE TO SELF: Give Gary and Tyler wedgies on Monday.

I skidded to a stop and walked my bike through the entrance gate. "What is it about sixth-grade boys?" I said, thinking aloud. "The way they glom onto stories about zombies and green ooze. They're a total mystery."

"The only thing that's a mystery is why Ms. Hinkel thinks it's okay to send us to this stupid cemetery," Toni said, pulling off her helmet.

"It's a school project. Trumbull students come here every year," I told her. Gary had mentioned that his older brother had the same assignment when he was in middle school.

"Let's just get this over with, girl," Toni said, setting her bike against the black iron fence. "I have better things to do than dust the dirt off some dead guy's tombstone."

I hung my helmet over the handlebars and leaned my bike next to Toni's. It seemed to disappear into the weeds that lined the fence. I was locking it up when I heard footsteps crackling through the fallen leaves. I shot a look at Toni. Toni looked at me like she was seeing a ghost.

"Hello?" I called out. Nothing. Just the footsteps.

Then a figure emerged from behind a tree. Gary. I breathed a sigh of relief.

He lifted the headset of his Walkman away from one ear. "Hey. Wassup?"

"We were calling you," Toni said with her hands on her hips. "Next time, remember your manners."

"You two having a fight?" he asked, swinging his backpack off his shoulder.

"No!" we both hollered at the same time.

"Okay, just asking," he said, closing a small notebook.

"Are you finished?" I asked.

"Not even," Gary said. "Good thing my family has roots here. The Williamses have been in Abbington since the beginning. We were the number-one black founding family. Back when they were laying the cornerstones here, the Williams family ruled."

Modesty is not Gary's strong point. Then I remembered that he was supposed to be paired with the Diva of Dance. "Where's Megan?"

He rolled his eyes. "Just my luck to get Megan O'Connor as a partner when she's swamped with another project."

"The party princess has gone AWOL on you, huh?" I felt a twinge of satisfaction that Megan wasn't doing everything perfectly lately.

"Yeah, she's all hyper about finding a place," he said. "But it's under control. My brother had this project a few years ago. No big deal. I don't need Megan to clean the grave. But I couldn't find the one I wanted to research. Anyway . . ." He snapped his fingers. "My brother says there's a primo section in the library on local history. Megan and I are going to check it out tomorrow."

"Tomorrow? Sounds good. We can meet you,"

I said, shooting Toni a look that said, "Don't even think about flaking on me." She just grabbed her notebook from her backpack and turned away. Well, it was one way to get her into the graveyard.

I said good-bye to Gary and followed Toni down a narrow dirt path that snaked among the trees to the tombstones.

"Don't ever be making dates for me," Toni said sternly. "And don't ever sign me up to work with you on a project again. You are way too bossy, Casey. Graveyards and zombie stories . . . just ask me to walk under a ladder and break a mirror."

"Toni, quit it with the superstitions and get your butt over here," I said. "I didn't pick this project."

"You were the one who had to zip right over," she said, looking at her watch. "Like these dead people couldn't wait another day to be adopted."

We walked toward the area that had the most plots and started reading the stone tablets. At first it was interesting. But after a while, all those "Beloved husband"s and "Devoted Mother"s started to sound like a bad greeting card. Besides, it was getting cold. Wind whistled through the cemetery. Why was it so much colder in the graveyard than it had been outside that gate? I shivered.

Then I looked up through the dense wall of trees. The sky was a smear of red and purple. The sun was starting to go down.

"Toni?" I said cautiously, realizing she'd be a total basket case if we stayed here till after dark. "It's getting cold. Let's just list some names and decide later what family to trace."

"For once, you have a good idea, girl," she said, moving some overgrown weeds away from a tombstone and taking out her camera.

We went from tombstone to tombstone. Toni snapped pictures and copied down names from the headstones. I whipped out my notebook and scribbled some details for my story.

Some headstones are large and grand, with inscriptions of art and poems. Some headstones just list a name with a date of birth and date of death.

Creepy trees sway in wind.

Weeds growing like crazy around head-stones, along the fence, on the paths.

A baby birch has grown through the

wrought-iron fence and wrapped around
a lamppost.

Some graves with plastic flowers, some
with dead real flowers.

Then I heard it. A strange noise. A—
Ccccrrreeeeaaaakkkkkk. . . .

"Man, this is so not cool!" Toni high-stepped
to where I was standing and grabbed my arm. "It
sounds like, like . . . like a coffin opening!"

I felt goose bumps on my arms as I listened.
My eyes scanned the graves . . . the fence . . . the
trees . . . the gate.

"Toni, it's that old rusty gate," I said, as confi-
dently as I could. "The wind is blowing it open
and closed. Really."

Still holding my arm, Toni glanced at the gate.
"Are you sure?" Her amber eyes were huge.

"Completely," I said. "Now let's just finish up
and go."

As Toni went back to writing down names
in her notebook, I spotted a tombstone I hadn't
seen earlier. It was beautiful. Ornate. With an
etching of a young girl in flight. She was flying forward, but looking back, with a hand out-
stretched.

ABIGAIL WILLIAMS
loving daughter
She wanted to see the world
Born 1888   Died 1899

"Check this out," I called to Toni. "She was only eleven years old when she died. Just like us."

"Excuse me?" Toni's crazy hair swayed as she shook her head at me. "I am not dying anytime soon."

"No, no, she was our *age*," I said. "Get real, Toni. This zombie talk is rotting your brain." I stepped closer to the girl's tombstone, which was made of pale pinkish marble.

What had happened to her? Why would . . . Then I heard something. A grinding sound. Unless Toni was having some dental work done in the graveyard, something strange was happening.

"That was not a rusty gate!" Toni whispered. She darted toward the gate, then froze. "It's a coffin. Someone's opening a coffin!"

I cut between the two grave markers to catch up with Toni. "It's nothing," I lied, trying to stay calm. Trying to ignore the sweat on my cold palms. "It's probably just an animal or something."

"Right," Toni snapped. "An animal, pushing its little animal coffin open."

Before I could answer, the grinding sound stopped, and we heard a *clunk*. Or was that the sound of my heart banging against my chest?

"CASEY!" Toni shrieked, pointing into the shadows.

I grabbed her as if she was a life raft.

CHAPTER
5

Girl Reporter Debunks Dancing Statue!

"It MOVED! It moved!" Toni yelled. She made a mad scramble toward the fence. I was pulled along, through mud and leaves. She probably would have dragged me right out of the graveyard, but the black iron fence blocked the way.

"What moved?" I yelled back. "What?"

"That angel!" She pointed to a statue just inside the gate. Even her shiny orange fingernails were shaking.

I was shaking, too. Not so much because of the statue. It was really Toni's freakout that freaked me out. But underneath the goose bumps, there was a part of me—the skeptical reporter part—that still didn't buy into a Purser haunting. A few funky noises did not a haunting make.

Breaking away from Toni, I inched toward the angel. Leaves crunched under my sneakers. Toni called me back, but I kept going. No way could I investigate a haunting without checking out unusual noises. I was close enough to see the crosscuts in the angel's wings. That's when it creaked, and moved again.

I stopped. I stared. Then I started laughing.

"Toni, this statue isn't alive. It's loose," I said, brushing a few acorns away from the base of the statue. "See, it's loose on its bolt. Look right here." Gripping the angel by its wings, I turned it around. It stuck for a minute, then spun back like a twirling ballerina. A twirling, creaky ballerina.

Not that the statue was designed to turn, of course. Someone might have been messing around with it. But a supernatural phenomenon? I didn't think so. I could see Toni's face relax a little bit. But she wasn't totally convinced.

"So what if it's loose," she said, hurrying over to grab her backpack where she had dropped it. "That thing turned to look right at me. It was watching me! I want to leave. Now."

I sighed. I was just about up to my freckled nose with Toni and her my-way-or-no-way boss-ing around.

"At least tell me how many names and shots you got," I said, as nicely as I could.

"Enough. Let's go."

But before she could march away from me, I grabbed her notebook and took a look. Her handwriting looked like a car wreck.

"How can you even tell what you wrote, Toni?" I asked. "Don't go thinking I'm going to do all the work for this assignment."

"Did I tell you to cork the lectures, or was I just talking into blank space?" Toni said, stepping so close to me that I could feel her breath.

"Blank space?" I said with as much vinegar as I could muster. Now I was mad. "The only blank space is going to be in your half of our report!"

Toni did not say a word. After we got on our bikes, she tore down Purser Lane in front of me as if she wasn't going to wait at all. Passing between rows of birch trees, I caught up to her and pedaled alongside, but she still didn't say a word. When we got to the block where we needed to split and go our separate ways, Toni stopped.

"I don't know who you think you are, Casey," she said. "But I won't be pushed around. I can't make it to the library tomorrow. I'm busy. All day."

How much attitude was I supposed to take in one day? "Toni," I said, trying not to sound as annoyed as I was. "We still have to do research and clean a grave. There's tons more work to do.

And we have to go to the library tomorrow because Ms. Hinkel made arrangements with the librarian—if you had been in class you might know that. How does two o'clock sound?"

"No good," she said quickly.

"Three then?" I asked, ready to scream.

"That's bad, too," she said looking at me like I was a supernag. "Actually, I'm booked all week."

"You're just too scared to go back," I said, with a look that could straighten her wild hair. "Admit it. Tough chick Toni Velez is scared!"

"So what?" She zipped her jacket up to the neck. "You're scared, too. But you're so bent on getting a story that you don't even care that the graveyard flips me out."

That derailed me. She was right. I did need to get my story. And I wasn't all that into being at Purser Cemetery by myself. Have I mentioned how much I hate to be wrong?

"Fine, Toni," I said. "I'll do the library legwork for our project by myself. We'll figure out when to visit the cemetery later. But this is the last time I team up with you. Ever!"

For a minute, I thought Toni was going to cry. Instead, her face hardened, and she just turned her bike and rode off.

I adjusted my backpack and took off in the other direction.

As I biked, I kept replaying the whole after-noon in my mind. I was so sick of Toni playing the attitude card with me. Why me? I treated her okay, didn't I? I didn't deserve to get blasted after every comment that came out of my mouth.

But there was something else. Not that she was ever my best friend. But recently she had been acting like I was the smelly kid on the bus that no one wants to sit by.

What did I ever do to her?

I pedaled faster and faster. If Toni didn't want to hang out with me, then that was just fine. Fine. FINE!

The sun finally set. Everything was coated in the purple glow of dusk. And the wind was a powerful gust now. I figured it must have swirled a lot of dust in the air, because my eyeballs were watering.

In case you were wondering why I was wiping my eyes all the way home.

Studies Reveal Surprise Inside Each Tootsie Pop!

I STUCK MY bike in the garage and walked into the warmth of the kitchen. Gram was boiling water.

"Are we cooking?" I said, peering into the pot at the rumbling bubbles.

"I was thinking about making some pasta," Gram said, holding up a bag of rigatoni.

"I'm impressed, Gram," I said. "What kind of sauce are you making?"

"Sauce?" Gram suddenly looked concerned.

"Yeah, Gram, you know, like tomato sauce or cream sauce?" I said. "To put *over* the noodles?"

Gram bit her bottom lip. As I said, cooking isn't Gram's thing. Writing is. You can't hold that against a person.

"No biggie. There's always butter and garlic," I said.

"No, there isn't." Gram peered into the fridge. "No butter."

"And the garlic is growing horns." I picked up the bunch of garlic from the windowsill and tossed it in the trash.

"Okay, it's burgers from Juicy Burger," she said, grabbing the phone. "You want fries with yours?"

"Awesome." I headed upstairs. "Slap some cheese on that puppy, too."

As soon as I walked into my room, I flipped on my computer. I had math and Spanish homework, but first I wanted to go online. That girl in the graveyard stuck in my head. Abigail Williams. She wanted to see the world, but she died.

I wanted to see what I could dig up on her.

I didn't find anything in the Abbington Library website under "Williams, A.," so I opened my notebook to look at the other info I'd copied from the graveyard.

Father: Henry Williams

Mother: Aurora Purser Williams

Brother: Jonathan Williams

I found a website that searched family trees and did a monster search. It took forever, especially since Williams is such a common name. I did find out that Abigail's grandfather was Artemis Purser, one of the town founders.

There the trail ended. Abigail died at eleven, which meant she never married or had any kids. That meant no descendants.

I exited the website and took another approach. Maybe if I found information on the town of Abbington, there'd be news about Abigail. How she died. How her family lived. I searched for half an hour, only to find zilch. The Abbington Library home page had a posting about how they were in the process of loading all their archived information onto their site, but they didn't expect it to be done for a couple of weeks. Somehow, I wasn't surprised.

Still, on my desk there was a stack of printouts from last night. Ghost sightings. Plasmic leftovers. Can you believe that some people believe ghosts leave a form of Jell-O behind? Rolling a few Tibetan riverstones around in my hand, I thought about my graveyard story. I already had the truth behind the moving statues. But would Megan go for it?

It was worth a try. I picked up the phone and punched in her number.

"Hey!" I said when Megan answered. "Did you ever hear about the haunted house on Long

Island? Every night, you can hear the ghosts of the original owners shuffling off to bed."

"Oh, Casey, it's you." Megan sounded disappointed. "I was waiting for the owner of Trumbull Lanes to call me back. They might have a cancellation."

"You mean for the yearbook party?" I asked. "A Halloween party in a bowling alley?"

"I'm getting desperate!" she said. "The party is supposed to be a week from today!" Her voice squeaked with an eerie quality that was unlike Megan. Was everyone I knew falling to pieces?

"Well, just wanted to let you know I'm making progress on my story. So you can spend all your energy freaking about the party."

Silence. Then she asked, "What story?"

"About the haunted graveyard. When Toni and I were there this afternoon, I figured out that moving statue. It's just this angel statue with a bolt that's loose. It swings around on its pedestal."

"Really?" Megan said flatly. "We'll talk about it Monday at the meeting. I mean, I'm glad you've found something. But I'm just so overloaded right now. There's the party. And the Day of the Dead project. So far, poor Gary's done everything. So let's put your story on the back burner till Monday, okay?"

45

Okay? What kind of answer was that? I heard the sound of a rushing wind. Megan was blowing me off.

"Wait," I said. "I've been doing research, too. And there's—"

"Casey, I've got another call. It's probably the bowling man. Gotta go!" And she hung up.

I stared at the phone. The Queen of Correct had hung up on me. I was tempted to call her back and bump the bowling man off the line, but I could hear Gram downstairs.

I found her in the kitchen, holding a paper bag that smelled like heaven.

"Were you talking to your computer again?" she said, yanking off her jacket. "You definitely need some brain food."

"Actually, I was talking to Megan," I said, reaching into the bag and stuffing about ten fries into my mouth at once. "Abow my soory."

"Now say 'Peter Piper picked a peck of pickled peppers,'" Gram said, snatching away the bag and bringing it to the table. Gram has this thing about sitting down to eat. Probably from eating on the run all those years when she was chasing stories.

I swallowed. "Sorry," I said. "Hey, Gram, maybe you can help. I need info on the history of Abbington. In particular, Purser Cemetery. Or this girl who's buried there." I explained the web sites I'd visited.

Gram nodded as she chewed her burger. "That can mean only one thing."

"What?" I asked. She looked so serious. "Did I miss something?"

"No, but the way I see it, you have but one last resort," she said melodramatically. "The library. Do you remember what it is?"

"Vaguely," I said, going along with the joke. But she was right. I didn't use the library very often. When I did go in, it was usually to log on to a PC. Not that I don't read books. Books have great stories in them. But for research, there's nothing like having the Internet at your fingertips.

"Books—they can be marvelous things," she teased. "But let me warn you: You have to turn the pages by hand—no scrolling. And proceed with caution. Pages will tear when handled too roughly."

"Oh, stop!" I said, tossing a napkin at her. I could do book research. Really I could!

When I got to Abbington's one and only public library on Saturday afternoon, it was already hopping with Trumbull students. Apparently they had as much luck as I did on the Net.

"This section is for reference only," the librarian

who led me to the local history section told me. "But you can copy anything you need. Too bad this project couldn't be delayed by a week or so. The Historical Society has been compiling this information for a website. They copied our materials years ago, but it's taken awhile to get funding. The site should be up and running by the end of next week."

"Just my luck," I said, eyeing the throng of students. If the Day of the Dead had come in December, I'd be doing one-stop research in my bedroom. I spotted Tyler and Ringo at a table.

"Hey, Barney," I said, patting Ringo's still-purple head.

Tyler smiled and held out his hand for a low-five. "Casey—what's up?"

I slapped his hand and held mine open for the return. "Hey." Were people watching? Could they see the sparks that shot up to the ceiling when Tyler and I were together? Or was that just another supernatural phenomenon?

"Where's Toni?" Ringo asked.

"Don't ask." I plopped my backpack onto the table and sat down.

A couple of kids at a neighboring table shushed us.

"*Shush* is *hush* backwards," Ringo said, writing the word. "Almost."

"Shhhhh!" they rasped, louder this time.

"Okay, okay," I said over my shoulder. "Who invited the chitchat police?" I was beginning to understand the attraction to the shush. Empowerment. The right to silence, with one harsh "Shush!"

I thought of Toni. She was probably at home, figuring out other ways to make my life miserable while I slaved at the library.

"It's not fair," I whispered to Tyler and Ringo. "Toni's backed out on me. Completely. She wouldn't even meet me here today."

"No way!" said Tyler. "Maybe you guys can cook a Mexican dish or something."

I shook my head. "We had a fight. I told her I'd work alone. Me and my big mouth."

"It *is* big," said the shushers, glaring at me. They collected their books and moved to a distant table.

"'Bye!" I called after them. "Come back soon!"

"Too bad," Tyler said, trying to help me feel better about Toni. "With two people it goes a lot faster."

"Thank you, Einstein," I said, rolling my eyes.

"Not Einstein, McKenzie," Ringo said, holding up a family tree diagram. "Tyler McKenzie's family is like the Kennedys of Abbington. There's tons of them."

I looked at the work Tyler and Ringo had done researching Tyler's family. They had a detailed family tree sketched out in Ringo's distinctive printing. And Tyler had four crumpled pages of a handwritten draft of their report outline.

To be honest, I felt jealous. Why couldn't I be almost done? And why didn't Tyler team up with me?

"Check this out," Ringo said, opening a big brown book to a yellowed page he'd marked. He pointed to a grainy photo of a place with all these men in overalls standing around. The photo caption said:

McKenzie Mill:
First business to employ men of color

"One of my ancestors owned this lumber mill that had black workers." Tyler rested his chin on his hand, looking at the book like it had magic powers. "People got mad at the owner, Robert Henry McKenzie Junior. They called the millwork slave labor. But the townsmen didn't realize that he was paying the workers. Plus he gave them a place to live behind the mill." Tyler raked a hand through his hair. "But people judged him without knowing the truth."

I stared at the old-time photo. If only pictures could talk.

"Things aren't always what they seem," Ringo said, tying a red bandanna over his head. Now he looked like a cherry Tootsie Pop. "Everyone just thought Mac Junior was this dude taking advantage of those men. And in reality something totally different was going on."

"So your ancestor employed former slaves?" I asked, suddenly wishing I had paid more attention in history.

"It's like when you go to a three-D movie," Ringo continued. "Without those glasses, it's just a movie. With them, you see what's really going on. *Terminator* is my favorite. 'Sa-rah Con-nor—'"

"*Terminator* wasn't in three-D." I scrunched my nose at Ringo. "Tyler? You were explaining?"

Tyler tapped his pencil on the big book. "Lots of runaway slaves came here through the Underground Railroad. You know, Harriet Tubman led them north."

"I wonder if they'd call the Underground Railroad a subway today?" Ringo said.

"Um, actually," Tyler said, looking at Ringo like he thought Ringo was on a sugar high, "the Underground Railroad was a network of people. They would hide slaves who were walking up from the South to freedom. They'd feed them, give them a place to rest for a little while. Thousands of people escaped. And Harriet Tubman helped about three hundred people herself."

"So Harriet was a conductor with no real train?" Ringo asked.

I could barely believe how much work these two had done. I started to stress. "You guys have some awesome research, and I have zip." I pulled my notebook out of my backpack. "I'm going to strangle Toni."

"Hey, solo artist," Ringo said, kicking me under the table to get my attention. "Maybe you need some three-D glasses to see the real deal with Toni."

That stopped me. "Like what? To see more of that 'tude coming at me?"

"Don't think like a molecule," Ringo said. "Maybe she's got something else going on. Something that doesn't have anything to do with you. It's not always about you, Casey."

He had a point.

"You know," Ringo went on, "like my hair."

"Oh, here we go again," Tyler said, leaning back in his chair.

"It's purple on top," Ringo said. "But underneath it's just brown hair. What you see isn't always what's there. Or vice versa."

I looked at Ringo like he had a tree growing out of his head. Was he right? Then I looked over at the cartoon he was drawing.

Was Toni weirding out about something that had nothing to do with me? Could I, Casey Smith, be so wrapped up in my own stuff that I'd missed the fact that my friend was wrapped up in something else?

Get real.

Dust Bunnies Deliver
Baskets of Eggs!

MY NOSE FELT like a big dust-bunny had crawled in and made camp there.

The books in the Abbington section were so old! And big. And long. And raggedy. And besides the books, there were files of old clippings and scrapbooks that people had collected over the years and donated to the library. I'd seen old things on microfilm before, but I'd never had the chance to pick up the actual yellowed clippings. The dry paper felt good in my hands. This was history. News that someone had treasured enough to save.

After Tyler and Ringo left, I got to work, searching for Abigail's name. I was in the library for so long that I was sure I could feel my hair growing. Then, in a clipping about local businesses, I spotted the name of Abigail's dad, Henry Williams. Turns out the family wasn't as documented as I thought because some members became Pursers through marriage. Henry married a Purser. Aurora. Abigail's mom. The Williams family was a lot smaller than the McKenzies.

I opened my notebook and started recording the few facts I found about Abigail and her family.

Henry Williams, wealthy industrialist. Made his fortune through the mines he owned.

Aurora Purser Williams, wife of Henry. Organizer of Abbington Women's League.

Abigail Williams, killed in a carriage accident. Part of her petticoat wrapped around the wheel. It pulled her from her seat in the carriage. Her head hit the ground. She was bedridden for three days, then she died.

Jeez.

There was a lot of information about a big mine, which was the original Purser family business, but not a lot about the family. It said that Henry was so grieved about Abigail's death that he let the business slip. He never really got over the accident. But except for the details of her death, it didn't say a whole lot about Abigail.

Another book repeated the same info, but it also had pictures: Henry and Aurora at the lake. Henry holding baby Abigail. Abigail and Aurora attending a Women's League tea dressed in fancy dresses and holding fancy umbrellas. Parasols.

I stared at Abigail's face. She was pretty. Her smile was sort of crooked, but it was a big smile. And she had brown hair. Like me. I wondered if we would have been friends if she was alive today.

Then, when I was ear-high in books, I heard a familiar squeal.

"Casey!" the voice squeaked in delight. "Gary said you'd be here." Megan.

"Hey," I said, with all the enthusiasm of a snail. I couldn't help but notice that Megan had on her studious library outfit: khaki pants, pink sweater set with matching pink-glitter bobby pins so she could read without hair falling in her eyes.

Megan pointed behind her. "Gary stopped at

the reference desk. We're almost done. Can you believe it? Gary did such a super job!" she said with so much pep I thought she might do a quick cheer.

"Super," I said. "I mean that." No, I didn't. Did I have to hear about yet another team that was doing a better job than poor, poor me?

Gary cruised over, nearly as perky as Megan. "What's happening, Casey?"

"Oh, just a mountain of research." I waved my hand like a T.V. spokesmodel over the stack of books.

"The reference lady said you had some books with Williams family stuff," he said, eyeing my books. "Can I take a look if you're done?"

I'd forgotten. He was Gary *Williams*. I was searching Abigail Williams. Different Williamses, of course. But same book.

"Here. I'm done," I said. "All yours."

Gary grabbed the book and started leafing through it. Megan sat down and started telling me Gary's family story. Great. She spread out a copy of Gary's family tree on the table and jabbered without taking a breath.

"His mom had this copy of their family tree," she said, like it was a map to a buried treasure. "The original is in their Bible, but the Bible is missing. Isn't it lucky she had a copy?"

"Yeah," I said, "really lucky." I should have such luck.

Then Gary slammed the book shut. "Nothing," he said, pointing to a spot on the tree. "This is the weird thing. We can't find information on my great-great-grandfather anywhere. And I know he lived here in Abbington, because he passed his house down to the family. My old uncle Arthur lives there with his three hunting dogs."

"I bet if we could find that family Bible it would clear this up," Megan said. "Where in the world could it be?"

"And check this out," Gary went on, opening up a big black folder that was lying on the table. "There are three reference files for my family in this library. But when you look in the 'Williams' folder, the documents are gone."

I couldn't tell if they were just unloading on me, or asking me my opinion. But when do I not give my opinion? Besides, I had already switched into my reporter mode. My nose for news tingled. Or was it that I smelled a rat?

"You guys," I said, raising an eyebrow. "Do you think those documents were removed on purpose?"

When I walked out of the library I felt like

a released prisoner. After sifting through old papers and trying to help Gary and Megan make sense of the missing things, I'd had enough of that place.

I was going to ride straight home to hug my computer.

I pulled on my helmet, set my Illusion 2000 on autopilot and pushed off with my Converse. I wanted to get home in record time and start working, since I was obviously on my own with this project.

As I pedaled, I started fuming. I wasn't okay with Toni bailing on me. I did want to see Ringo's side of things. The truth was, it was totally possible there was something up with Toni that I didn't know about. But right now all I could think about was how my whole day was shot doing the work of two people.

I got home and put my bike away in the garage. Then I heard something. Or someone. In the backyard.

I quietly took off my backpack and set it silently down by my bike. Then I slinked along the wall of the garage to the open door. I was trying to look out without being seen, when I spotted it on my back porch. A massive poof of curly, red-streaked hair.

Toni's hair. Hair that could take over the planet.

She saw me, and her eyes widened. For a minute, I thought she was going to fly through the air and pounce on me. Instead, she ran across the lawn and pounced on me. "Casey!" she yelled, squeezing my arm. "Am I glad to see you!"

"You . . . glad?" I guess I was a little shocked. I mean, was this the same Toni who never wanted to see Casey Smith again? The same Toni who yelled at me outside school?

"Listen up, girl," Toni said, grabbing her backpack and fishing around in it. "When you look at these, you are going to wig out! They are insane!"

She handed me a folder filled with photographs. As I pulled them out, she talked a mile a minute. "I developed these last night after I got back from the cemetery," she said, pulling her knees into her chest and hugging her ankles. "Check these out."

I looked at the pictures. And I was instantly spooked.

The photos showed something unusual in the graveyard. I couldn't tell what it was. I flipped through a few more photos. It showed up in all of them. It was like a haze. A whitish fog kind of haze.

Then I looked at the last photo. It was a

picture of me by Abigail Williams's grave. And there was something floating above me.

"Can you believe it?" Toni gasped, squeezing my arm. "It's the ghost!"

Camera Captures What Naked Eye Can't See!

"PURSER CEMETERY *IS* haunted," Toni said, doing a triple finger snap in the air. "I knew it!"

I studied her cautiously. "For a girl who's scared of this stuff, you're surprisingly psyched."

"It's proof!" she exclaimed.

I wasn't sure. "First of all, the whitish haze could have happened during developing. And the thing that's floating above me? It's not exactly a ghost. It's like a ring."

"A halo, girl," Toni said, smacking her gum. "It's a halo sure as my name is Antoinette."

"Your name is Antoinette?" I was suddenly distracted.

"Yeah," she said with a smirk. "You think Toni comes from Anthony?"

"I just didn't know that," I said, staring at her. "How did a Mexican-American girl get a French name?"

"My mom digs French stuff, okay? Just deal with the pictures, girl." She pointed at the photos. "Look at all the halo thingies. In every one. I say it's an angel. Or a spirit. Or a ghost. Whatever you want to call it, it's real."

"I don't know," I said. It was a lot to swallow.

"Casey, remember that statue that spun around and stared at me? It was an angel. A spirit that can't rest. *Abigail's* spirit."

"Now you're getting carried away, Antoinette," I said. "That theory is pretty far-fetched."

"It's not," she said, her wild hair flying in the breeze. "This is what people truly believe happens on the Day of the Dead in Mexico. So she's a few days early! Maybe she screwed up her calendar or something. She's the walking dead, and I'll bet she's got a message. Maybe she's trying to zap us. Maybe she's just a sad spirit because she died so early. But you've got to admit, she's as real as the freckles on your nose."

I still was not convinced, and I don't like to be reminded of my freckles.

"And," Toni went on, "only my mom calls me Antoinette, so watch it."

"What kind of film did you use?" I asked, holding up the photos. "Maybe the processing solution went bad."

The smile faded from Toni's face instantly. "You think these photos are one big mistake?" she asked. "You think I used bad film and then I screwed up while I was developing that bad film? I'm just the dumb picture-girl? Is that it?"

"Toni . . . no, of course not," I stammered. "I'm just trying to cancel out every possibility, that's all."

"Cancel all you want, but that's Abigail's ghost," she said, snatching the photos out of my hands. "She's an angel who has a reason for allowing us to know she's there. She needs something. Or someone." She glanced through the photos, smiling.

I looked over her shoulder. I had to admit, some of the photos were intriguing. There were distinct halos around me at Abigail's grave. There were also halos floating near her parents' graves. It was spooky, that's for sure. But there was something fishy about it all.

Then I thought about my story. The photos would be just right to run with a story about ghosts.

GIRL REPORTER INTERVIEWS GRAVEYARD GHOST!

"I died too young!" ghost claims. "Just let me have fun! I never tried pizza, skateboarding or Nintendo!"

Okay, I needed a lot more to make it into a story.

But it was nice to have Toni not acting like she hated me. I wanted to thank the grouchy gods that she wasn't in a terrible mood. For once. She was actually excited about this. For the first time in days, she wasn't treating me like I was the human equivalent of a science project. I stepped back into the garage, grabbed my backpack and pushed the button to close the garage door. Toni was leafing through the photos again, mystified by the "angel."

Call me crazy, but I decided now would be a good time to see if there really was something bothering Toni. "Toni, can I ask you something?"

"You can ask. It doesn't mean I'll answer," she said.

Her answer got under my skin. "See, this is exactly what I mean," I burst out. "You're being mean to me, and I've had it! Something is up with you, and I want you to tell me what it is. Now."

Toni tucked the photos into her backpack.

"Who do you think you are?" she said, making a face that looked like she'd just taken a bite of something rotten.

I wasn't backing down. "I'm the girl who's been your personal punching bag," I said. "You've been nothing but nasty to me, and it's horrible. Totally uncalled for, Toni."

"I'm leaving, Casey," she said, turning toward her bike.

"You are not!" I hollered. I clasped her arm in my hands and pulled her toward the back porch. "You're staying right here!"

Toni scowled at me. "What did you say?"

"I said you're staying. You're stuck here until you tell me what the problem is." And I meant it. I pointed toward the porch, dropping my pack on the ground.

Wonder of wonders, she climbed up and sat down on the top step. Then she sighed.

I put my hands on my hips. "You were saying?"

"Okay, okay," she said, looking at her nails. "Ms. Vermont wants to set up a meeting with my parents next week. You happy now?"

Ms. Vermont is the school counselor. It's not usually a good thing to get a call slip from Ms. Vermont.

"What did you do?" I asked.

"Nothing. Forget it," she said, putting her backpack on her shoulders like she was going to try for another getaway.

"Please, just tell me, Toni," I said, holding my ground. Getting Toni to open up is tougher than chewing a trampoline. Jeez.

"Did you fail a test?" I probed. "Did you get caught with answers on your wrist? Did you bite some poor unsuspecting girl's head off because she called you Antoinette?"

I was relieved when Toni laughed at that last question. At least she could still laugh.

"Seriously, Toni," I went on. "My life would be a lot better if you just told me why you hate me so much."

"I don't hate you, Casey," Toni said, looking worried. I couldn't tell for sure, but it looked like she was ready to cave. "I really don't. Sorry if I've been a little edgy lately."

A *little* edgy? Her personality could cut glass.

"If you really want to know, I'll tell you," she said, turning the bangles on her wrist around and around. "But this has to stay between you and me. Completely secret."

I gave her my scout's honor. Even though I had never been a scout.

"Okay, here's the deal," Toni said, wrapping a long curl around one finger. "My family moves a lot, so I never took any of those achievement tests. You know the ones?"

I did. Those tests were about as much fun as getting a cavity filled.

"Well, I sort of slipped through the system because I was always switching schools," she went on. "Then Ms. Vermont made me take some stupid test. Now she says I have an LD."

"LD?" I squinted.

"Learning disability," she said, still twirling her bracelets. "I've got this thing called dyslexia."

CHAPTER 9

Girl Reporter Refuses to Publish Source's Secret!

"DYSLEXIA? SOUNDS LIKE a car of the future," I said. "The Dyslexia Three-Fifty Turbo. For all your interplanetary travels!"

Toni was not amused. "It's serious, Casey," she said. "Ms. Vermont says there are different kinds of symptoms. But mine is that I have trouble writing. I can read fine, but forget spelling or handwriting."

"There's a bright side to this, Tone," I said, and I believed it. "Maybe your brain is making up for the spelling thing and that's why you're good with pictures."

For a minute, I thought I had perked her up. Then her face fell again. "A lot of good that does me if I can't even graduate from middle school," she said.

69

I had no idea it was this serious.

"This is really embarrassing. But I guess I needed to tell you, 'cause we have to do this assignment together. I mean, you were probably going to figure it out, after you looked at my handwriting."

I didn't want to admit that I was far from figuring it out. My mind had been wrapped around my story, not around Toni's problems. But I did remember thinking that her notes were a mess. "What's with your writing?"

"Um, see . . ." Her amber eyes flashed with an odd intensity. Pain? Or fear. I wasn't sure. "They say my spelling and writing are at a fourth-grade level." Then she was silent.

I didn't know what to say. But I was thinking that this could happen to anyone.

"Kids are going to tease me, I just know it," she said. "I bet they're going to think I'm stupid. Especially when Ms. Vermont sets me up with some teacher in the resource room. The *resource* room! That's for dumb kids!"

"Listen, girl," I said, talking like her. "No one is going to accuse Toni Velez of being dumb. You're one of the sharpest knives in the drawer—and everyone knows it."

Toni was as smart as anyone I knew. But this sure explained why she was ready to knock my block off when I teased her about her writing when we were in the cemetery. As for our assignment together, that was another story. I wanted to help her, but if I did all the work she'd get zero out of it. Not to mention that it would be double work for me.

"Here's an idea," I said. "I can help you with our social studies assignment. But if I'm going to write the report, you've got to come through and do your share."

"What?" she asked.

"You do the presenting," I said. "Standing up in front of the class makes me sweat buckets. Plus, we have to go back to the graveyard." That last statement sat between us like fish odor. I could see the graveyard fear creeping back into her eyes.

"I know you're scared," I said. "But we still have to clean Abigail's grave for school. And I still have to get a story for *Real News*."

"I'm not scared. It's just that I have respect for the dead. The *walking* dead. You saw the photos!" She patted her backpack like it was a pet dog.

"You're scared of a statue that moves in the wind, and a squeaky old gate?" I asked. "Besides, if it's Abigail's ghost, as you say, she's probably a nice ghost. She was our age when she bit the dust. Maybe she's trying to reach out to us for a

71

special reason." Did I believe any of this? To be honest, I wasn't exactly sure. But it was calming Toni down.

"All right, all right, it's a deal," she said. "But only if you promise not to tell anyone about my . . . situation."

"I promise," I said.

"You have to swear," she said. "With a hand on your heart. I don't want my problem becoming a *Real News* headline."

I put my hand on my chest like I was pledging allegiance to the flag. "I swear I will not tell a soul." I can keep a secret. I can!

We decided that Toni should spend the night at my house so we could work on our project. We went inside to clear it with Gram and with Toni's parents. After she got the go-ahead for a sleepover, I figured something out that had been a big question mark in my mind for a really long time. No wonder Toni flipped every time someone suggested that she write a story. Often she had great ideas, but she backed off when we suggested that she write them up.

Now her reactions made sense. She had trouble writing. I mean, duh!

I smiled to myself. I was so glad that this whole Toni-the-Tiger thing was over. A few hours ago, I was her most hated person on the planet.

Now I was her confidante and partner. Maybe even her friend.

Things sure can change fast. Even in a town where the most exciting thing is a dead girl in Purser Cemetery.

Girl Reporter
Interviews Tsunami!

IN TONI'S HONOR, Gram had a pizza delivered.

While Toni washed her hands, I spotted the Saturday newspaper on the counter. I leafed through it, skimming over a story about a broken bridge. Thrillsville. There was also a story about a woman with twenty-seven cats. Freaktown.

Then my eyes lit on the Purser name. It was an ad for "Pumpkin-Picking at Purser Farms." There were pony rides, a hay maze, jack-o'-lantern carving classes and all kinds of food. It didn't sound half bad. And it was right next to Purser Cemetery.

"You know," I said, "Ringo mentioned this yesterday at lunch." Toni walked over and read over my shoulder. "The Trumbull cheerleaders are having a booth for apple-bobbing. But he didn't mention that it was at Purser Farms. Maybe we should go check things out. Wanna?"

Toni gave me the hairy eyeball. "I smell a Casey plan brewing. What's cooking, girl?"

"Well, I was wondering who owns Purser Farms. I mean, maybe the owner is related to the original Pursers. And Abigail. Who, by the way, is our adopted relative."

Toni sighed. "Leave it to you to choose the one spirit who pops out to haunt us."

"I know how to pick 'em," I joked as Gram opened the pizza box. "Ooh, pepperoni. Let's eat."

At first Toni was quiet around Gram. Wonders never cease. But Gram has a way of making people comfortable. By the time we were digging into our third slices, Toni was giving me a hard time about wanting to get back to Purser Cemetery.

"How much sense does that make?" she said. "You saw the ghosts in that picture, and now you want to go back even more."

"Excuse me?" Gram interjected. "What ghosts? Where?"

"Halos, not ghosts," I said.

Toni dug into her backpack and showed Gram the pics.

"I still think you're loco," Toni said. "It's like, here comes a giant killer wave. Everyone else in the world runs away from it. Except you. You run to the beach with your notebook and start asking the wave questions."

Gram laughed. "She's got you nailed, Casey. But I must admit, I understand that feeling. Sometimes you're itching to know what's really going on. Are you sure this haze didn't happen while you were developing the film?"

Toni raised a perfect eyebrow at me. I felt proud that I had the exact same reaction to the photos as Gram.

"No," Toni said, a touch defensive. "Anyway, I say you got an itch, you scratch it. You see a ghost, you run."

"Excellent point, Toni," Gram said, setting the photos down and stealing a piece of pepperoni from the box.

After dinner we took Toni's bag upstairs. I led the way to my bomb of a bedroom. "'Scuse the mess."

Toni dumped her stuff and plopped down on my bed. "Nice use of color," she said. "Like, every color. And cool pillows," she said, hugging one.

"The pillows are from China. Those shadow puppets are from Indonesia. My bedspread was woven in Peru. And this is a piece of the Berlin Wall," I said, handing her a chunk of concrete.

Toni turned it in her hand thoughtfully.

"What's the Berlin Wall?"

"It used to be a wall dividing people in Berlin, in Germany," I explained. "It was a symbol of oppression."

"Who put the wall up?" Toni asked.

"The Soviet Union," I said. "After World War Two ended, they took over half of Berlin. To make sure people wouldn't or *couldn't* leave, they built the giant wall. Families and friends were separated. But it didn't work. When the Soviet Union collapsed in 1989, the wall came down. The whole world celebrated. Gram was there. She says that chunk is a symbol of freedom."

"Rock on," Toni said, winking at me. She rubbed a smooth part of the cement. "So where's all this dirt you dug up on Abigail?"

I sat down in the computer chair and took my notebook out of my backpack. "So far it's just notes. Nothing written yet."

While Toni looked over my scribbles from the library, I thought I might investigate a different subject: dyslexia. It only took a minute to zip over to a website, after all. No confusing Dewey Decimal system to deal with. No waiting to get onto a computer. And no annoying "shush"es from people who can't stand the sound of air when they read.

I found dozens of sites on dyslexia. Most were

pretty clinical and confusing. But then I found one that was just for kids with dyslexia. It had this voice that called out: "You're not backward! You just read that way!"

"Hey, what's the deal?" Toni looked up. "Are you still working on the project?"

"I was curious," I admitted.

Toni grabbed a stool and pulled up next to me at my desk. We scrolled through all kinds of stuff about people with dyslexia: symptoms, ways to get through school if you have it. Everything.

"I already did some online research," Toni said. "But there are a trillion websites, and they all say different things."

"I'm getting that," I said. "It looks like they can't really define dyslexia. Not a cut-and-dried definition, anyway."

Gram says a good reporter takes all the information and narrows it down. She says sometimes I'll feel like I'm swimming in research. Like now. But a reporter has to boil down to the nitty-gritty, most important, easy-to-understand facts. Easier said than done.

I tried to nail the key points.

Dyslexia: difficulty in learning to read and write.

Sufferers are called dyslexics.

Most dyslexics have one or more of these problems:

* Difficulty in learning and remembering printed words
* Letter reversal (b for d, p for q)
* Number reversal (6 for 9)
* Changed order of letters in words (tar for rat, quite for quiet) or numbers (12 for 21)
* Leaving out or inserting words while reading
* Confusing vowel sounds or substituting one consonant for another
* Persistent spelling errors
* Difficulty in writing

"I've seen this before," Toni griped. "But it's more serious than a short list of stupid symptoms."

I nodded. I couldn't imagine having a hard time with words. For a reporter, words are modeling clay. You build them up, pare them away, make new formations. I wondered if there were any dyslexic journalists.

Toni rubbed her forehead. "Last year I practically wore myself out studying, just to scrape by with Cs so the counselors would leave me alone."

"That really bites," I said, scrolling through a whole bunch more gibberish about dyslexic doctors.

"One institute has a doctor who calls dyslexia a gift, which is just a joke. Some gift! I might as well drop out right now. Before everyone finds out and writes me off as a dumb loser."

"Oh, get over yourself, Antoinette!" I said as I scrolled through the site. "You are not dumb. Or a loser. And you know it. Look right here: Tons of famous people are dyslexic. And who's at the top of the list? Tom Cruise."

"What do I care about a guy my mom thinks is cute?" Toni said. "The guy is ancient. Isn't he, like, thirty or something? And if you don't stop calling me Antoinette, I'll stick my gum in your hair."

"I'm not telling you to put the guy's poster in your room. But he was eleven years old at one time. He had to learn how to read so he could read a script, right? Someone figured out how he could learn, and he did. Same goes for other dyslexics. Including you, Gum Girl."

"Yeah, we can learn," Toni complained. "In special ed. Like the resource room. Hand me the dork hat!"

"Toni . . ." I faded out as I read through the info on the screen. "Here's the one from the doctor who says it's a gift. Oh, and here's why."

Toni slumped in her chair.

"'Often dyslexic students have a better understanding of three-dimensional objects,'" I read from the screen. "'They think in pictures instead of words. Many renowned artists are dyslexic.'"

"Good thing I've got a camera," Toni said. "If I didn't have my shooter, I'd be Toni Velez: Loser Squared."

She was slumping, pouting, complaining. All things I have never associated with Toni. This dyslexia thing was really hurting her. Not sure what to say, I picked up a pen and scribbled down a few notes from what I saw on the screen.

"Hold up, Casey!" Toni was suddenly breathing down my neck. "What's up with you taking notes on this?"

"For one thing, I always take notes," I said, twiddling my pen. "For another thing, this is something kids need to know about."

Toni folded her arms and gave me a look that could boil the skin off a chicken.

"Look, Toni," I said, "I'm not going to tell your secret. But this might be a story. A good story. How many students are out there having a hard time and don't know why? They could be dyslexic, too."

Toni lowered her chin and glared at me like a bull ready to charge. "Casey Smith, you swore you wouldn't tell anybody!" she hollered. "And now you're taking notes for a story. The exact opposite of your promise!"

"I swore I wouldn't tell a soul that you have dyslexia. And I won't," I said, not really getting why she was so mad. "Why would anyone connect you to a story about a learning disability?"

"People who know you and know me might!" She was really fired up now. "And excuse me, Reporter Vulture, but if someone has a reading problem, they don't read *Real News*. Duh! And who are *you* to advertise my problem to the school?"

"I am not advertising your problem to the school," I said. "*If* I do a story, and that's still an *if*, you won't be mentioned. I won't tell anyone on staff. Or anyone at all. You won't be anywhere near this story, Toni. Seriously, you need to calm down."

I turned my back on her and typed in the address to a website about the supernatural. I figured changing the subject might cool her jets.

Toni sat back down. "Okay, okay. Let's just get this project done," she said. "If you don't run your mouth off, I won't freak out."

"Amen, Antoinette," I said. "And if—"

Then she flicked my ear. Hard.

"Hey!" I grabbed my throbbing earlobe.

"You wanna call me Antoinette again?" she asked, squinting down at me.

"No. You win. Jeez," I whined. "That hurt."

She pointed to a link on the screen she wanted me to click on. "Start writing, Word Girl."

So I did. Using the tiny bit of info I'd found on Abigail, I scrawled out a very short description of our "adopted" relative.

Toni researched on the web and found groovy clip art to add to our report. She found a carriage and a wheel and an old-fashioned miner's lamp. It was almost fun. We were a team. Almost friends. I wondered if this was what it was like to be Megan. She has so many friends. Girl friends.

I'm such a boy's bud. Griffin and Ringo are my best friends. I've never had a close girl bud. But Toni was a lot more like me than I'd thought. She could ride a bike over mud and rocks. She didn't giggle and clap tiny baby claps at the mere mention of a teen heartthrob. If it wasn't for those crazy orange nails, she'd be just like me.

Bottom line, I was glad to have Toni at my house.

"How's it going, girls?" Gram walked in.

"Almost done," I said, swiveling around to see her. "Except for the stuff on Abigail. It's all about her dad so far."

"I vote we just stick to her dad," Toni said, packing up the notes. "There's too much information missing on Ghost Girl."

"Let's just see what we find tomorrow," I said. "Oh, Gram, I've got a new strategy for finding some Pursers." I told her my idea to go to the farm and see if we could find any Purser descendants.

"Nice angle," Gram said. "I'll drive you over. I want to get a pumpkin, if a zombie doesn't get me first. Now grab those pillows from your bed and we'll get you set up."

Downstairs in the den we spread sleeping bags in front of the TV and got cozy with some cookies and milk.

"Your gram is great," Toni said, dunking a cookie into her milk. "But what's the deal about a zombie getting her? What did she mean?"

"Toni," I said through a mouthful of cookie. "Like a zombie is really going to get us on a hayride in front of a hundred people? Get real."

Boys and Ghouls Laugh Their Heads Off at Zombie-Fest!

"ZOMBIES SURE KNOW how to throw a party," I said as we pulled into the dusty, crowded parking lot at Purser Farms the next morning. It was warm for October, and the sunshine had lured people out. "Just look at this place."

It was like a circus. A circus with a Halloween theme.

There were scarecrows on every fence post. Fabric ghosts hung from every tree. Pumpkins carved into toothy jack-o'-lanterns grinned from their eerie outposts. And all the workers were in costume. Gruesome ghouls, zombies, witches and vampires wandered through the haystacks and booths.

For Abbington, this was screaming excitement.

"Oh, great," Toni said. "Now we won't be able to tell the real thing from the workers."

"Focus," I said, yanking on her sleeve. "We're here to find a real live Purser."

We watched people clamber onto the hay truck to go out to the pumpkin fields. I went up to the skeleton at the front of the line and asked him who owned the farm. He didn't know. He was just a high-school kid, working for the weekend. He pointed me over to the mummies on the other side of the stables.

We passed the little kids getting rides on ponies. Beside the barn, two people wrapped in gauze were making poodles out of balloons for squealing four-year-olds. I could only make out a pair of brown eyes amidst a sea of bandages as I asked one mummy if any Pursers were still connected to the farm. The mummy told me, "It's a different owner now, but they kept the name."

"I'm looking for someone in the Purser family," I said. "I need to interview a descendant for a school project."

"No Pursers that I know of." The mummy's eyes stared off into the distance. Then he nodded. "But talk to Rusty. He's the zombie running the main concession stand. If anyone knows, he will."

A lead. Straight from the mummy's mouth.

I thanked the mummy as a group of kids ran past, shrieking and laughing, chased by a vampire.

"Let's go find the main zombie man," I told Toni.

"I'm with you, girl," Toni agreed, giving my arm a friendly pinch.

"Are you still wigged out by all this?" I asked.

She shook her head. "I'm cool, but you guys have no respect for the dead."

On the way to the food stand, I spotted Ringo. He was standing behind a table in a section of booths that the farm rented to community groups.

"Hey, Casey!" Ringo waved us over. "What's up, Toni?"

"The hair on the back of my neck," Toni said, slapping him five. "This place is wacked."

"Isn't it?" Ringo said with a huge smile. "Wanna buy a brownie? Or how about a pumpkin muffin?" He waved a hand over platters of brownies, cupcakes and cookies.

I picked up an oatmeal nut cookie and fished a quarter from my pocket. "I thought you said the cheerleaders were having an apple-dunking booth."

"We were," he said, flicking the latch on the cash box. "But Jamie Papasergio's mom said it would be a waste of food. So now our booth is a bake sale booth."

"Don't let Gary see you selling cupcakes," I

said. Gary was having enough trouble dealing with Ringo as a dude cheerleader. I figured Ringo in the kitchen would throw Gary completely over the edge.

"He's been here, done that," Ringo said. "He bought like twenty cupcakes for the guys on the team. I think they're washing cars or something. But dudettes, have you heard? About the graveyard?"

I hate it when someone else has news before I do. "What about it?" I asked.

He leaned in and whispered: "Do *not* go there today. I'm serious." Then he looked toward the cemetery, which was one field and one ravine away from the main farm.

I wanted to wave him off, but it's not every day that Ringo says the words *I'm serious.* "What's the deal?" I asked.

"It's haunted," he said. "I was there with Tyler last night to clean graves, and gruesome stuff happened. I'm going to tell Ms. Hinkel on Monday. Maybe she'll cancel the assignment."

"Ooh." Toni smiled. "That's the best idea I've heard all week."

"Wait a minute," I said, reaching across the table to tug on Ringo's sleeve. "What happened exactly? And what possessed you two to go after dark?"

"It wasn't dark when we started. We just wanted to get the assignment done. But after we pulled the weeds, we started hearing these weird sounds. Moaning and scratching." His gray eyes were huge, like two full moons. "Then there was a bright light. So we called out, 'Who's there?' But nobody answered. Then we heard more noises. And the light was getting closer. It chased us out of there."

"I knew it!" Toni said, holding both hands up like she was cheering a touchdown. "I told you, Casey. That cemetery is haunted."

Eerie sounds? A bright light? I didn't buy it. Not as a haunting, anyway. But it made me that much more itchy to get there. "Listen, Toni," I said as Ringo turned away to wait on a customer. "Consider the source. Ringo and Tyler? They've always believed the legends about Purser. So they went there expecting to hear stuff. Don't let these guys get you all worked up over the wind."

"I don't know," she said, looking toward the cemetery. "I don't like it."

"So what's new?" I said. "I'll check it out just as soon as we do some digging about Abigail. It's broad daylight. No worries."

"Speaking of daylight, it's actually warm today," Toni said, pulling her big hair back. With a tug and two twists she formed a perfect pony-tail, which she tied off with some thingie from her pocket. "Let's get something to drink."

First we bought two cups of icy apple cider. Then we sprang for some gourds to decorate Abigail's grave with. Toni liked the colors, and the price was right—eight for a dollar. While Toni was paying for them, I went over to Rusty, an old guy who looked like he'd just dug himself out of the ground.

"Purser descendants." He rubbed his chin as he mulled it over. "Well, you know the cemetery is managed by Putnam Properties. They have an office on Main Street."

I pulled my notebook out of my backpack and wrote:

Putnam Properties

Toni winced, staring at the worm that was sticking out of a hole in Rusty's hat. Clearly, she did not dig the zombie gig.

Then Rusty snapped his fingers and said, "You want to talk to Sunny Bellmore."

My nose began to tingle—the scent of a story. I rubbed it with the back of my sleeve. As Rusty the zombie spoke, I added these notes:

Ms. Sunny Bellmore, Purser descendant!!!

Nursery school teacher

Runs pumpkin-painting booth

Rusty pointed us to a tent with a fat happy-faced pumpkin sitting by the door. We thanked him and headed over.

But Sunny Bellmore wasn't so easy to find. A woman dressed like a witch told us she was on break.

"Witches get breaks?" Toni asked as we stepped out from the shade of the booth back into the bright autumn sun. "What, are they unionized?"

Just then I spotted Megan getting out of the family van. Two little blond Megan clones were tumbling out behind her as she hurried over to us.

"There's Megan," Toni said, tugging on her ponytail. "And the Meganettes."

"Hey, you two," Megan called to us, waving a manila envelope. "Is this gorgeous weather, or what? My mom brings us here every year to pick pumpkins, but I'm supposed to meet Gary. Have you seen him? I got some super research for our project."

"He's washing cars," I said, eyeing the envelope. "What's that about?"

"My dad got it," she said, opening the clasp. "He knows a guy at the Historical Society who's working on the Old Abbington website. Anyway, this is going on the website, but Dad got him to make a copy for us." She held up a sheet of paper. It was a map divided into rectangles, with a legend written by hand.

"What is it?" Toni asked.

"A legend for the black section of Abbington Cemetery," Megan said proudly. "We've been having so much trouble tracking down Jacob Williams, I figured this would solve all our problems."

"Did I hear 'Williams'?" Gary asked, joining us. Beside him was his friend Ken Ford, a tall, African-American kid who's also into sports.

"Williams . . ." Gary went on, "the name on everyone's lips. Usually preceded by 'the Great Gary.' Or 'Amazingly Athletic African-American All-Star.'"

"Ego check," Toni told him.

"I got it!" Megan told him, waving the map. "Dad picked it up this morning. But I still can't find your great-great-grandfather's name."

Ken held one corner of the map. "This is cool. My ancestors must be on here, too."

"Probably," Gary said, leaning over Megan's shoulder. "But we're looking for my guy, Jacob. See? Here's the Williams family plot. Here's

Franklin and Maxwell and Sarah. . . ."

Megan was shaking her head. "No Jacob. I've been staring at it since I got it."

"But Jacob was the first member of my family to live here," Gary said. He pointed to the graveyard. "If his body isn't buried over there, where is it? Will you tell me that?"

We all exchanged puzzled looks.

"A missing body?" Toni was wigging again. She clamped her hands over her ears. "I don't want to hear this!" She backed away and sat on a picnic bench.

But I stayed. My nose was itching. This was a story. "A missing body," I repeated. "From how many years ago?"

"Try a hundred and forty," Gary said.

I sighed. "If no one's found it in all those years, our chances are not good," I said. "But I do like the mystery of it."

"It's no mystery! It's a mistake," Gary insisted.

"It's not a mistake," Megan countered. "This is a copy of an original document from 1902. If it's not on here, that means . . ."

"Hey, can I get a copy of this?" Ken asked. "My great-grandad is right here."

I left them to piece things together. Personally, I liked the missing body theory better than an administrative error.

"I wonder what happened to poor Jacob Williams?" The question niggled at me as I sat down beside Toni.

"I don't want to know. Just as long as he doesn't come walking around while I'm in the graveyard," Toni said, crossing herself.

I checked my watch. "Look, we've got time to kill before Sunny comes back from her break. I'm going to check out the cemetery. Meet me back here in twenty-five minutes."

"Excuse me?" Toni lifted an eyebrow. "Do you think I'm going to hang around here alone with wannabe vampires and ghouls jumping out of the woodwork? Not to mention a body missing from that graveyard over there?"

I shrugged.

"Besides, you can't go to that cemetery alone." She found her shades in her backpack. "Look, if I have to go back there for more photos and whatever, we might as well do it now."

Whoa. This was the Toni I used to know and fear.

Moving away from the crowd, we found the road to the graveyard. It grew more and more quiet as we got farther away from the fair. Except that Toni was chattering nervously the whole way.

"Okay, you clean the grave and I'll snap the pictures. We just need to do Abigail's grave,

94

right? Or maybe we should do her father's, too. Just in case we can't find enough information on the ghost girl. Is this just the most stupid assignment you ever heard of? I mean, this is not the way it's done in Mexico. You do not adopt a stranger just because—"

Ahead of us, beyond the cemetery gate, the bushes moved.

Toni grabbed the sleeve of my jacket and pulled. "What's that?"

It was only some kids, like us. Another group of sixth graders.

"Hey, you guys see anything unusual?" I asked.

"No," three of them answered at the same time. "No floating girls or moving statues. We did bump into a zombie, but he was cool," one kid said with a goofy smirk on his face.

Toni glared at me, and I shook my head. "Sixth-grade boy humor," I said firmly. "Come on."

"Just hurry, Casey," she said, following me to Abigail's plot. "There were also five of them, and there are only two of us."

Toni pushed up her shades and adjusted the settings on her camera. "I don't see the halos," she said as she snapped photos. "Do you think only the camera lens can pick them up?"

"No idea," I said. I knelt down beside Abigail's

grave and listened. The graveyard was silent and still. It smelled of damp earth and leaves—the smells of autumn.

Toni lowered her camera to glare at me. "What? What are you waiting for?"

"I'm just listening for the sounds Ringo mentioned. Do you think he heard the gate? Or maybe a statue moving in the wind?"

"Just pull the weeds and cork it," Toni ordered. "You don't want to be here when Abigail comes out to pick up her gifts."

"Actually, I do," I muttered.

The earth was wet under my knees. I brushed a few leaves from Abigail's gravestone and started pulling out tall grass from around the edges.

Toni went over to the fence to get a close-up of the angel with the loose bolt nearby. Then she straightened and looked over her shoulder.

"Do you feel that? Someone is watching." She hurried to my side, shivering. "I can't shake the feeling."

"The only thing I feel is the mud under my nails and the wet knees of my jeans." I stood up and tossed a clump of dirt and weeds over the fence that ran along the perimeter of the cemetery.

"I'm serious," Toni said, backing up for a new angle. "It's probably the spirits. They're annoyed at being disturbed in their resting place. Kids have been here all day bugging them, and they're totally ticked. And when they pop out, we're the ones they'll blame."

I felt a sudden chill, but I didn't know if it was from Toni's words or the fly that grazed the back of my neck.

"Would you just zip it and keep snapping?" I said. "I've got the grave under control." I put my backpack on the ground and took the gourds out. Resting an orange-and-green bumpy one against the headstone, I wondered why farmers grew plants that were basically useless. "What's the deal with a gourd, anyway? Do people ever—"

Creeeaaaaak.

"Eeyiiii!" Toni's camera swung around her neck as she darted to my side. "What was that?"

Then we heard a scratching noise. A loud scratching noise. And a howling. Like a moaning wolf.

"It's zombies! Zombies!" Toni shrieked. "They're scraping their way out of the ground!"

I didn't know what to say. To be honest, I was shaking a little, too.

But I didn't want to panic. Not yet. "It's okay," I said quietly. "You stay here and I'll check it out."

Toni backed against the fence.

My heart was pounding in my chest as I stepped forward, then paused. Where should I go?

With the noises echoing through the graveyard, it was hard to tell where they were coming from.

"Aaaoooo!" I heard a howl that gave me goose bumps.

"Casey! Casey! Oh my gosh! LOOK!" Toni wailed.

I was ready to tell her to shut up. She was only making it worse. But as I looked over she leaped forward, as if someone had just tried to grab her feet.

"CA-SEEEEEY!" she screamed.

You've never seen anyone move so fast. I bolted over to her like a bullet.

She was staring into a huge hole by the fence. I guessed we'd missed it before, because it was covered with dead leaves. Dead leaves that were now churning, as if a wind was kicking them up from under the earth.

What was in that hole? What could possibly make the leaves move so crazily? A speedy mole? A giant earthworm? My heart was about to pound right out of my chest. There was only one thing to do.

"RUN!" I yelled.

"I . . . I can't!" Toni stood and clutched her camera, staring at the ground, as frozen as the tombstones around her. "There's a—a HAND!"

Girl Reporter Snaps Photographer Out of Daze!

A HAND? I stared into the hole of swirling leaves. Yes, there it was. Gray fingers, reaching, clenching the air.

A hand was emerging from under the ground.

My instincts kicked me right in the butt. "Run—now!" I took hold of Toni's arm and pulled. "Come on!"

I dislodged Toni from her freeze. She nearly fell onto me, then took off. Her long legs kicked up leaves as she tore through the cemetery. I wasn't far behind her.

It's not every day you see a corpse reaching out of its grave. I have to admit, on the scare scale, this would have made Buffy run for cover.

We ran all the way back to the farm. When we

were close enough to hear laughter and voices, we slowed to a walk.

"Are you okay?" I asked, out of breath and sweaty.

Toni was shaking like crazy. "No! I'm pretty far from okay. I'm lucky to be alive."

I thought that was extreme, but I bit my bottom lip to keep from saying anything. Toni was upset. She needed sympathy. She found it at the bake sale booth.

"Ringo, you were right!" Toni yelped. "We saw the zombie! His hand was reaching up! Another minute, and he was going to pop right out of his grave! I can't believe I'm still alive to tell you this."

"No way!" Ringo's gray eyes were lit with excitement.

"And the noises," Toni went on, pressing her fingers to her temple. "Like a howling wolf! It was so awful!"

"So you heard it, too," Tyler said, cruising up with Melody.

Right behind them were Megan and Spence the Politician. He's president of our student council. For an eighth grader, he sure spends a lot of time around Megan. "Poor Toni," Megan said sweetly. "Calm down and tell us what happened."

Toni pointed toward the cemetery. "A zombie

nearly climbed out of its grave over there! Casey saw it, too."

"I did," I admitted. "I mean, it was a hand, all right." I replayed the scene in my mind. How could it be? There was no such thing as a zombie or ghost or ghoul. "Maybe it was an electronic thing. What's that called?"

"Animatronics," Tyler answered.

"It was a zombie!" Toni was practically spitting nails.

"I thought Purser was haunted by a ghost," Ringo said.

"Zombies. Ghosts. Walking spirits! Call it what you want," Toni said, waving a manicured nail in the air. "The dead are awake . . . and they don't sound happy at all."

"Sounds beastly," Melody chimed in.

Megan turned to scan the crowd. "I don't want my little sisters to hear this. They'll be so frightened!" This from the girl who didn't think the graveyard story was news.

"So you see how this story hits?" I told her. "Like a tidal wave over an island."

The Princess of Priss nodded, her blond hair bobbing. "Oh, yes. You were right about that, Casey."

Music to my ears.

Toni kept moaning. "I can't stop shaking.

Somebody get me a drink, will you?"

"Right away," Melody said, rushing off to the snack bar.

"Oh, man!" Tyler nudged Ringo. "We could've died there yesterday!"

"Yeah," Ringo agreed. "Freaky City. And a zombie is the mayor."

I spun on my hightops and left them standing there by the cupcakes. There'd be time later to brainstorm about what that hand might have been. I wanted to go back to the graveyard and check out the hole—with some kids to keep me company, of course. But at the moment, I had work to do, and Toni was a little too weirded out to help me. I headed straight for the pumpkin-painting booth to find Sunny Bellmore.

The same witch was there. She directed me to another witch helping some kids paint their mini-pumpkins. I recognized the girls. Tiny blond elves. Megan's little sisters.

"Ms. Bellmore?" I asked.

The witch turned and smiled at me. "Yes?" she asked. Sunny Bellmore had one of those open faces: high cheekbones, broad smile, light blue eyes. She gave off one of those helpful vibes. Just what I needed.

"My name is Casey Smith," I said, reaching for my backpack. It wasn't there. That's when it hit me. My backpack, my notebook—all my stuff was sitting on the ground beside Abigail's grave.

That sealed it. I was going back to the cemetery, just as soon as I finished this interview.

I told Sunny Bellmore about the social studies project and about needing to find out about Abigail Williams.

"I may actually be able to help," she said. "I have a box with some old family items you can look through—a Bible, and a few mementos that have been handed down for years. And I think there's something of Abigail's. A poem or something like that."

I made a plan with Ms. Bellmore to meet her here after school on Tuesday. What a score! I was so excited to finally have a connection to Abigail. I went over to the bake sale table, where Toni was sitting back, eating an apple from a bag Ringo was passing around. She seemed happy that I'd gotten a lead on Abigail. Not so happy about going back to the graveyard.

"No way," she said. "I know we're in this project together, but one encounter with the walking dead is enough for me. Case closed."

"But my backpack," I said. "My notebook. My house keys. Gram is going to be ticked off."

"Get someone else to go with you." Toni folded her arms. "Sorry, Casey, but a girl's got to know her limits, and I'm over mine."

I turned to Ringo. He shrugged. "I'm stuck here for the next half hour. I'll go with you as soon as I get off."

"Okay," I said, shoving my hands deep into the pockets of my jeans. I felt sort of naked without my backpack. "Meet me over there, by that wall of hay."

"It's a maze," Ringo said, tossing an apple to me. "Don't get lost."

At the moment, lost sounded good. I needed some time to sort this stuff out.

With fresh apple in hand, I wove my way to the back of the hay maze. I stopped at a quiet spot that reminded me of a house of hay. There was a hay bale to sit on. A little hay table. Even tiny holes like windows in the wall of the hay maze. The afternoon had cooled off, and I just wanted to eat my apple and chill out for a minute.

I decided to play the question game. Sometimes when my mind is jammed, brainstorming is the only way out. Sliding the toe of my sneakers over the dirt, I wrote:

NOISES

What would make howling noises?
A giant wolf.

Scraping noises? A bulldozer.

Then I wrote in the dirt:

HAND

If that gray hand didn't belong to a zombie, what was it? A Halloween prank? Some mechanical hand left there by some kid? If that was true, why hadn't it moved when we first got to the cemetery?

I closed my eyes and chewed my apple. Was I missing something? I tried to remember the cemetery, the sounds and sights in that moment that Toni spotted the hand.

Suddenly, something snaked around my waist . . . and pulled!

My eyes flew open as I screamed.

CHAPTER 13

Scientists Confirm Sixth-Grade Boys Have Absentee Brains!

I TRIED TO wriggle away. I clawed at the hands and pounded the arms that had shot right through the tiny hay windows.

"I'll kill you even if you're already dead!" I screamed.

Then I heard the laughing. And the hands let go. I turned around and climbed onto the hay chair to look over the maze.

Tyler McKenzie.

"Tyler, I swear I'm going to kill you!" I said, slugging him in the arm.

His answer was just a sweet smile. Of course, whenever he smiles, I see that crooked tooth that gets me every time. But what was he thinking, playing another prank on me? Or maybe he wasn't thinking at all. Further proof that sixth-grade boys have moments of total brain lapse. Was he behind the hand prank, too?

"Hey, wait a second! Were you the one trying to scare Toni and me in the graveyard?" I asked him.

"No. No way!" he said, getting serious. "I wouldn't try to scare you for real!"

"Oh, not for real. Just for a goof!" I stepped over the top of the maze and dropped down to the ground beside him. "If I had a bad heart, I'd be a goner. Nails in my coffin."

"It was just a joke," he said sheepishly.

I felt bugged. And not just at Tyler. At this whole Fright Night vibe that was going around. It was so *Outer Limits*. So fantastically stupid. And it was contagious.

Contagious. What if that was what the graveyard-haunting thing was about? One kid pulled a prank and got lots of attention. So another kid pulled something else, and caused a stir. So the pranks went on. And on.

Whether it was a copycat thing or the same kid, I felt sure I was onto something. I needed to search Purser Cemetery for leads. "I've got to go back," I said aloud.

"Home?" Tyler asked.

I shook my head. "The cemetery."

Tyler pretended to punch numbers into his

palm and speak into a cell phone. "Hello, Zombie-land? Dig a grave for Casey Smith. 'Cause she's lost her mind."

"Don't try to talk me out of it," I said, pinging his arm. "I left my backpack there. And unless you want the nickname Prank Boy for the next year, you'll come with me."

He lifted his arms and muttered in a mono-tone: "Zombie see, zombie do."

I laughed as we headed off around the edge of the pumpkin field.

"So what's the plan?" Tyler asked. "We spot zombie, we run?"

I shook my head. "We snag backpack. We gather clues. We need to comb the hole where that hand popped up. I would've done it before, but Toni didn't feel like hanging around."

"And were you going to give the hand a low five?" Tyler asked.

I wasn't going to admit I'd been scared. At least, not to a boy.

When we got to the graveyard, I paused. The grounds were starting to look so different. More than half of the graves had been cleaned by sixth graders, and the decorations made it look sort of like a shrine. Some kids had placed flowers and papier-mâché skulls by the tombstones. The place was shaping up, skulls and all.

My backpack was just where I'd left it. Relief washed over me as I checked my notebook and zipped up the pack. A reporter can't afford to lose her notebook.

"So where's the hole to Zombieland?" Tyler asked.

I led him over to the spot by the fence. "Start digging, Prank Boy."

He kicked at the wet leaves. "You're asking me to scrape out a hole in a graveyard?"

I nodded. "Just stop if you see a gray finger."

We lifted armfuls of dank, moldy leaves out of the hole. When we had most of the leaves out, we saw how the gray hand had disappeared. At the bottom of this hole was a tunnel. A short tunnel, with sunlight showing a few feet away. The hole went down, under the iron fence. And it was big enough for a kid to squeeze through.

"You know what this means," I said.

Tyler rubbed his nose with the back of one dirty hand. "The graveyard is infested with giant groundhogs?"

I smiled. "This is a way in and out for . . . whoever. Like this." I slid my legs under the fence, gripped the bar above me, and slid through. I found myself on the other side, which was hidden by shrubbery. Of course, I was now covered with muck and dirt, and I probably smelled a little undead, too.

Tyler popped out behind me. "Maybe the zombies use this path to get back to their graves," he said.

I was ready to smack him. But then he smiled at me, obviously joking, and I saw his crooked tooth. I could never stay mad at him.

"Very funny," I said, stepping forward to slug him. Instead, I tripped on something hard. I looked down. It was a large, flat rock. And the black iron fence next to it had scrape marks.

"Well, well, well. What do we have here?" I asked, bending down. I dragged the rock along the scrape marks on the fence. Sure enough, it made a weird grating noise that echoed through the cemetery.

"That explains that chilly scraping sound," I said, inspecting the mystery rock. "Guess it's not zombies scratching out of their graves, after all."

"Yeah," Tyler said, bending down to pick something up. "And it looks like the zombies get cold out here at night, too. Check out this old glove."

He tossed it to me. It was an old glove, all right.

An old *gray* glove.

I pocketed it. My first real zombie clue.

Fraidy Cat Mentalities Cloud Judgment!

THE GRAY GLOVE was burning a hole in my pocket.

I was itching like a rash to show my new evidence to everyone on the staff of *Real News*. When I went back to the farm to meet Gram, Gary and Megan had already left. So I saved it overnight. What a great way to start a Monday, if I do say so myself.

I walked into the newsroom and dropped my backpack on Dalmatian Station.

Everyone was still buzzing about yesterday's scare at Purser.

"Anyone who goes back to that place needs major therapy," Toni said while filing her nails.

"Or they just need to check for evidence," I said, pulling the glove out and holding it up like a flag. "Exhibit A, one gray glove. Ladies and gentlemen of the Fright Club, Purser Cemetery is *not* haunted. You are all victims of a stupid boy prank."

Everyone leaned in to get a closer look.

"Stupid *what* prank?" Gary asked. "Who says it's boys?"

Toni frowned at the glove. "That is a glove. I saw a peeling, smelly zombie hand."

"I hate to zap your drama, Toni, but this is what we saw rising up from that hole." Tossing the evidence on the table, I told them that the hole was really a tunnel leading outside the cemetery.

"And who says that glove wasn't left there by a gardener or something?" Megan added.

"The landscapers come only four times a year—not last weekend. I called their offices first thing this morning," I said, glad to be a step ahead of the pack. "Besides, you saw how it looked before the kids cleaned it up."

Ringo picked up the glove and inspected it. "Is this going to be another lime-green sock hunt?"

"Remember how you jumped to conclusions about *that*?" Megan said.

They had a point. When school first started, someone stole a math test and sold it to a girl in lime-green socks. I saw the whole thing. Well, I saw the socks. I had lots of theories about the whos, whens, and wheres. And I got a couple of people in big-time trouble.

So I'm not perfect. Who is?

"Let's not go there," I said. "This glove—"

"One glove does not make a fake zombie, Casey," Megan interrupted.

"I second that motion," Gary said, raising his hand as if he was in a Senate meeting.

"First of all, she didn't make a motion," I snapped. "Second of all, she's wrong. I mean, I saw this glove coming out of the leaves. It was the perfect zombie-hand disguise. Right?"

"Like you know what a zombie hand looks like?" Gary prodded. "Don't tell me you dug up some zombie dirt on the web."

"You are missing the point, totally," I said.

I was so bugged that they weren't ready to rally around and tell me how brilliant my amazing theory was. They were all believers. Believers in everything that goes BOO! Their fraidy-cat mentalities were clouding their judgment.

I couldn't sit there listening to them put down my new evidence. I closed my notebook and grabbed my backpack.

"Casey!" Megan called after me. "What about—"

"I'll pitch my stories at lunch," I said, ducking out the door. "I'm getting a monster headache." At this point, even the halls of Trumbull Middle

School were better than bogus stories about Purser zombies.

Unfortunately, the halls of Trumbull were also buzzing with zombie-speak.

"Casey Smith!"

The girl, Eleni Milewski, who was yanking my arm was in my math class. She's always getting busted for talking when our math teacher, The Terminator, is doing problems on the board. And she's a major fluff ball. "I heard from Sarah Jacob who heard from Dan Sandinetti who heard from a girl who knows this guy in Toni Velez's P.E. class that you were almost bitten by a dead zombie!"

Eleni reminded me of one of those windup toys. Was she serious? But then more kids came up to me. Word was going around about a zombie giving Toni and me a hand.

At first I wanted to paint my forehead with: "We did not almost die! Zombies do not exist!" But the stories the kids were telling me weren't just about me and Toni. They had their own tales of ghost sightings and strange events at Purser Cemetery. All kinds of freaky stuff. And all within the past few days.

Some kids had seen a ghost girl swaying in the trees. Two other kids were so freaked by the noises that their parents were making them switch projects—they had to bake Mexican cookies instead. One boy was there alone and heard a moaning voice tell him to "get ouuut."

I thought about Toni's photos with the hazy halos floating above Abigail's grave. I'd been so sure this was all one big prank. But suddenly I wasn't so sure anymore.

What if the entire school was *not* suffering from mass delusion? What if the ghosts were real? Well, if the sightings were real, I could document them. Would that make a huge story, or what?

At lunchtime, I headed back to the *Real News* office. If I wanted to get a byline, I had to pitch my stories. Megan and Gary sat at Dalmatian Station, leaning over a few pages of marked-up copy.

"Another story on Trumbull's drooling, dribbling basketball team?" I asked Gary.

"I wish," Gary said, pulling on a baseball cap. "Sports are easy. Life is hard."

"It's our social studies project. We're still stuck on Jacob Williams," Megan said, not looking up from the copy. She circled something and scribbled a note in the margin.

"Our report's full of holes, and the body is missing," Gary said.

"No one can believe he's not buried in Purser Cemetery," Megan added.

Gary scratched his head with his pencil. "My father remembers visiting his grave there as a little kid," he said. "So what happened between then and now to make the grave disappear?"

"Grave robbers?" I suggested. This angle had potential.

"Do grave robbers steal tombstones, too?" Gary asked.

I shook my head. "Not in the pirate books I've read." I sat on a chair beside Gary. "You know, this is shaping into quite a little story. If the body was stolen, you should write it up. It'd make a great companion piece to my graveyard story."

"Which story might that be?" Megan asked, glancing up at her clipboard. "We slated this week's stories this morning, when Mr. Baxter sat in, after you took off."

It had sort of slipped my mind that Mr. Baxter had to approve all of our stories. He's so hands-off that sometimes I forget he's supposed to be there.

I opened my lunch—a turkey sandwich and carrot sticks. "Come on, Megan, I've only been talking about it since last week. So I missed the pitch meeting today. Don't ask me to grovel. It's not a pretty sight."

Megan reached for a peanut-butter cracker and held it up to stave me off. "Save the grovel, spare the appetite. We did leave a spot on page one or three for your graveyard piece."

Whew. "Excellent," I said. "Especially since Zombieland seems to be on everyone's mind at the moment."

Tapping a pencil against the table, Megan nodded. "Just be careful in that graveyard."

"Yeah," Gary said, standing up and gathering his papers. "And you'll let me know if you come across any extra bodies, right?"

"Next zombie I meet, you're the first kid I call," I said, pointing a carrot stick at him.

"Why does that not make me feel better?" Gary said. He slung his backpack over his shoulder and headed out. "Later."

"I'm going to get my dad to talk to his friend at the Historical Society," Megan called after him. "Somebody's got to know what happened to Jacob."

Gary just shrugged and walked out.

For a second I wished I was on the Jacob Williams story. But I, Casey Smith, girl reporter extraordinaire, knew better than to trounce on another writer's story. Instead, I thought about my other angle.

"There's one more story I wanted to pitch for this week," I told Megan. "Dyslexia," I said, like I was announcing "And the Oscar goes to . . ."

"The learning disability?" she asked.

I have to admit I was impressed she knew about it. "Yeah, it's a big deal for some kids," I pitched. "They might not even know they have it. It could help a lot of kids that are having a hard time in school."

"Hmmm," she hmmmed. I hate it when she hmmms me. "Could you just make it an editorial? I know I usually do the editorials, but I'm overloaded this week."

"Listen, Megan," I began. Writing editorials did not thrill me.

"It's just this party!" she blurted out. "I've tried *everywhere*! This town is just too small. There's nowhere left." She was nearly in tears.

I couldn't even look at her, she was so pathetic. Like a wilting pink flower. I eyed the glove on the table. The dirty old gray glove . . .

"Hey, Megan," I said. "Have you called to see if you could have the party at Purser Farms?"

She perked up instantly. It was like I'd blown happy dust in her face.

"Wow!" she squealed in delight. "That's a great idea! Do you think they'd let us? I didn't . . . Thank you *so* much, Casey!"

It looked like she was going to come around the table and hug me, so I grabbed my lunch and my backpack and headed toward the door.

Megan called down the hall and thanked me four more times for the Purser idea. "You may have saved the entire party!" she said cheerfully.

Now that was a scary thought.

Ringo caught up to me at my locker.

"Spacey Casey," he said, leaning on the locker next to mine. "I'm glad you opened the coffin on the haunted graveyard story."

Finally. Someone was appreciating my journalistic integrity.

"If it wasn't for you and that glove, my costume wouldn't be as groovy as it is," he said. "Oops, there's the bell. Later, alligator."

He was glad I was a bulldog reporter because it helped his costume?

"Hey!" I called down the hall at him. "What about *Real News*? Journalism. Kids have a right to know what's happening!" But he was already at the doors and halfway to Jupiter.

Candy corn was rotting everyone's brain!

I was surprised at first when Toni didn't show up for social studies class. Then I remembered that today was her big meeting with Ms. Vermont and her parents. Duh!

Ms. Hinkel started the class by talking about how some kids had been frightened at the graveyard. "That is not the purpose of this assignment.

While I'm not canceling it, I am advising that anyone who feels at all uncomfortable in the graveyard should not go there. If it's not for you, make a Mexican dish."

I leaned back in my seat. Maybe it was a good thing Toni wasn't here. Given the choice, she'd have us whipping up tortillas and tamales in no time.

That reminded me. Toni and I still had our appointment with Sunny Bellmore to look over that old Purser family stuff.

After school, Toni was still nowhere to be found. I headed to the newsroom to see if anyone had seen her.

Megan was writing in her notebook. Definitely something about the party. Probably how much pink glitter to buy for her costume.

Gary and Ringo were checking out their reflections in the windows, trying to get Ringo's new pointy ears to stay on. They were the biggest rubber ears I ever saw.

"What's up, Mr. Spock?" I asked, strolling over to the dynamic duo.

"I just keep *hearing* things," Ringo said, turning his head back and forth so we could see the massive ears. "Is it loud in here?"

"You are so fried," Gary was admiring his work on Ringo's head. "But you look fly."

"Yeah, fly like he's going to flap his ears and fly away," I said.

"Like Dumbo," Ringo added, touching his head.

"Dude, did you just call yourself dumb?" Gary joked.

Then we heard Toni at the door. "I'm the dumb one around here," she said.

She chucked her backpack on Dalmatian Station and flopped into a chair. I couldn't believe it. Tough chick Toni Velez had been crying!

"You had your meeting?" I whispered. I didn't want to alert the room that I knew something they didn't.

"Bad news," Toni said loudly. She obviously didn't care if everyone heard her. "Ms. Vermont says she's pulling me out of some of my classes to work with a specialist in the resource room."

"The resource room?" Gary said. "That's for—"

"Just say it!" Toni interrupted. Then she really started crying. "It's for morons!"

"Toni, don't talk that way." I put my hand on her shoulder. "Really. This is just so they can figure out how they can teach you."

"Yeah, teach me in the resource room!" she wailed. "At least you're off the hook, Casey!"

"Off the hook?" I asked. "For what?"

"My secret! Now everyone's going to know that I'm stupid!"

Girl Reporter Opens Mouth, Fire Shoots Out!

IT WAS THE loudest silence you ever heard.

Ringo took off his ears and sat in front of Toni. Megan folded her hands and looked at Toni with concern. Gary walked behind her and started rubbing her shoulders.

And me? I opened my big fat mouth. "This is no big deal," I said. I meant to say "This may feel like a big deal now, but—"

Toni slowly raised her head. "Casey Smith, are you out of your—"

"Wait! Wait!" I stammered. "That's not what I meant to say. What I meant to say was, this is a big story—" Oops.

That brought her to her feet. "Have you lost it, girl?"

If I'd never really believed that Toni would

kick my butt, I believed it then. I wanted to tell her how the research says she's going to be fine. I wanted to tell her how she shouldn't be so ashamed of the resource room. I wanted to tell her a lot of things. But I was nervous. And, as usual, my mouth was going before my brain was in gear.

I lowered my voice. "It's a done deal, Toni. You're going to have to trust me. I won't mention your name."

"Trust yourself. I'm outta here," she said, picking up her backpack and heading to the door.

"Toni," I called. But she was around the corner. Splitsville.

"Whoa," Ringo said. "That was intense. So, is dyslexia contagious? Because I keep getting this twinge in my leg. Every time I do a double backflip at cheerleading practice. Do you think I have dyslexia?"

"No!" Megan and I barked at him, in unison. At last we agreed on something. "It's not contagious, Ringo," Megan said more gently.

"Yeah," Gary added. "But why is Toni so freaked about it? My brother has it, and it's no big deal. In fact, I used to get jealous of the way my parents made such a huge deal over him. It was like, Brandon this and Brandon that. Toni should get what she can out of her parents. Major sympathy."

"I don't know about that," Megan said. "However, dyslexia is quite common. So I've read."

However? Quite common? What was she, a walking website?

But ranking on Megan wasn't going to help the real problem. Toni was freaking. And there was nothing we could do to help.

I couldn't sleep all night. I was thinking about my argument with Toni. Things had been going okay. We'd actually had fun when she'd stayed at my house on Saturday. How had all the wheels fallen off, just when we were beginning to roll?

When I got to school the next morning, I was tired. I plodded down the hall to the newsroom, my red Converse sneakers squeaking on the tiles.

Megan was there. On time, as usual.

"Here, read this," I said, handing her my front-page story about the graveyard haunting.

The night before, when I couldn't sleep because of Toni, I wrote the thing. And I have to say, I impressed myself. Again. It was loaded with anecdotes about other hauntings and details of the rumors about Purser Cemetery.

"Where's the real story?" Megan asked after reading my masterpiece.

"Come again?" I asked. "What do you mean, *real* story?"

"It's got all these 'TK's in it," she said, looking at my story like it stunk.

"TK means 'to come.' Duh," I said. "It means some details are coming soon.

"I know what TK means. But Casey, there aren't enough facts here for me to even start editing," she said, tossing it on the table. "You keep this. And when you get some solid stuff, get me a rewrite."

"A rewrite?" I was offended. "This thing is great right now. Don't be so picky."

"It's my job to be picky," she said, going back to her notebook. Was she dismissing me?

I was ready to launch into full reporter attack mode. But I just turned and marched out of the room.

I hate it when Megan O'Connor is right.

Time Capsule Opened, Moths Fly Out!

I WAITED ON the front steps of Trumbull for Toni after school.

Of course, she was late.

Megan's mom was taking her to Purser Farms to finalize her plans for the party. She'd been squeaking about it in the newsroom, so I'd asked if Toni and I could tag along. Believe me, sitting in a car with the Sugarplum Fairy and her Sugarplum Mother is not my favorite way to spend an afternoon. But I needed to meet with Sunny Bellmore and look at that family stuff. And it's a long ride on a bike all the way to Purser.

Megan emerged from the double doors of the school and stood above me. "Is she coming?" Megan asked.

"How should I know where she is?" I answered. "I'm not her boss."

"Jeez, Casey," Megan said. "What did I ever do to you?"

"You were born," I said, picking some dirt from under my fingernails. Sometimes I can't fake it with Megan. She's so . . . Meganish.

"Well gosh!" Megan said, slumping on the step next to me. "That's just not nice at all."

I thought about saying something fakey and sweet to make her feel better. But I didn't. Taste the real world, Megster. It's just not nice at all.

"I mean, why is it my fault Toni's late?" she asked.

Before I could whip off an answer, Toni was behind us.

"I was in the stupid resource room meeting my stupid new teacher getting my stupid new schedule," Toni said flatly.

Megan stood and touched her arm. "Toni—"

"Oh, don't give me that look, Megan," she said, yanking her arm away. "I'm not dying. Just stupid."

I stood and adjusted my backpack on my shoulders. "Okay, Einstein," I said, thinking maybe a new approach to Toni's prob might do her some good. "Ready to get to work?"

Toni just pinched her lips together and looked away.

Just then Megan the Prequel pulled up and honked. The horn made an ah-ooh-gah! sound. The pleasant woman behind the wheel waved at us cheerfully. I forced myself to smile back. Looked like perky was hereditary. I hoped it wasn't contagious.

After suffering through a Megan conversation about whether or not to have apple-dunking at the big party (give me a break!), we rolled into Purser's dusty parking lot and piled out of the van. Megan took off to squeak at the event-planning lady. Toni and I headed for Sunny Bellmore's pumpkin-painting booth.

A handful of little kids sat around one of the tables, laughing and patting their pumpkins. Ms. Bellmore moved around the table, handing out smocks and paintbrushes. "Hi, Casey, who's this?" she asked, looking at Toni.

"This is my . . ." I hesitated. "This is my *friend* Toni. We're working on the project together."

"Great!" She nodded at the kids. "I have to get these painters set up, but you can help yourself." Then she pointed to the back of the booth. "The box is right over there on the last table. Just be gentle. Some of the documents are quite old."

I was so curious about that box, my palms were sweating. Toni was into it, too. I could tell by the light in her amber eyes as she opened the top of the cardboard box and peered inside. It was the first time in twenty-four hours that I had seen a look on her face that wasn't a big bum-out.

"Bingo," Toni said, unfolding a sheet of paper. "Could we be any luckier? It's an old family tree. Just what we were missing."

"Oh, man, this is so perfect!" I said, taking the paper and inspecting it.

Toni was still digging through the box. "Hey, what's that?"

Under an old Bible and some yellowed papers, I caught a glimpse of faded red velvet. I gently picked up the old documents and the Bible and set them aside.

Carefully, I lifted out an old, ornate box. It looked like a jewelry box to me. It was square and just a bit smaller than a shoe box. It had beautiful tarnished silver edges and patterns carved in the dark wood. The old worn velvet was padded around the edges of the top, to make a frame on the top of the box. But nothing was in the little frame. Just a flat square of unpadded faded velvet.

Toni and I could barely breathe as I lifted the box out and set it on the table.

"Look, there's a little key," Toni said, reaching into the cardboard box.

The dark metal key was old-fashioned, like one in a cartoon. It had two teeth, and it had a heart-shaped loop at the other end, with a faded gold tassel hanging from it.

I put the key in the lock and slowly turned it. We heard a click, and the lid lifted about a half an inch.

"It's like a treasure chest!" Toni whispered. "Open it!"

I gently lifted the lid open, and a sweet little tune played.

"Can you believe this still works?" I asked, touching the velvet on the underside of the lid. There was also an oval mirror with faded velvet poofing all around it.

Inside the box was a faded lemon-yellow ribbon with another key on it. The key was tiny, and beautiful, and I guessed the ribbon might have been worn as a necklace.

Then there was a stack of letters. Old, old, old letters with the word "Dearest" written on the envelopes in the fanciest handwriting I'd ever seen.

"Do you think this is Abigail's stuff?" Toni asked, gently taking a letter from the box and holding it like it was a made of glass.

"There's only one way to find out," I said, taking out another letter. "You go first."

Toni turned the envelope over. It wasn't sealed. Gently, she pulled the letter out, unfolded the fragile paper and read:

Dearest Abigail,
My fondest wish is to be with you, my child. But since I cannot, I send you my most sound advice. Read, my darling. Sharpen your mind. Learn from your teachers. You bring yourself and those you love much happiness when you better your mind.
Fondly, Father

"Wow, it *is* her box," Toni said, folding the letter and slipping it back into its envelope. "That's so sweet I could just cry. But isn't telling her to read strange? Even I read. And I'm stupid, remember?"

"Actually," I said, ignoring the last thing she said, "a lot of girls didn't go to school. Back then, a lot of people didn't learn to read and write." Gram had told me about the olden days when women weren't supposed to do anything but get married, have kids and clean house.

"It's so cool that Abigail's dad wanted her to learn about things," I said. "I like him already. And, by the way, Einstein, you read that letter flawlessly. Get over yourself."

"Yeah, yeah. But reading is okay. Writing is the big booger for me," Toni said, looking back into the box. "Hey, look, there's something else here."

Toni pulled out a piece of paper that was folded in half. It was Abigail's personal stationery, with a design like paper lace across the top, and a big A below the lace in gold script. At the bottom was a pattern of faded yellow flowers. The paper was so soft, it was almost silky. Like a handkerchief.

Books I have read:
The Adventures of Sherlock Holmes
Black Beauty
The Adventures of Huckleberry Finn

The list went on. And on. It covered more than three pages. "Looks like Abigail really listened to her father's advice," I said.

Then I saw something in the box that looked like a piece of newspaper. I opened it so fast, I almost tore it along the fold.

"It's an old story," I said, reading the first couple of lines. "I think it's from . . . wait, oh here it is. *McClure's* magazine. Wow, it's dated 1895."

"Way old," Toni said, leaning in to look at it. "What's it about?"

"It's a story by Nellie Bly about her around-the-world trip," I said. "Do you know anything about Nellie Bly?"

"She was in that section we studied about women in history."

"Right." Jeez. I needed to start paying better attention in school. I scanned the clipping. "She went around the world and apparently wrote about it." I thought of Griffin traveling off to Europe. Then I remembered about Abigail and traveling. "Hey Toni, remember Abigail's gravestone said she wanted to see the world?"

"Yeah, I think so," she said. "It's hard to remember, since I'm always in a life-or-death situation when I'm at Purser."

"Don't start," I ordered. "What's that other piece of paper?"

Toni took out another piece of Abigail's stationery from the box and carefully unfolded it.

"It's a poem," she said. "By Abigail."

The bee who buzzes on the African plain,
The cold gray wet of London rain,
I am the bird who waits to fly.
One day I'll soar to distant skies.

The snake who slithers on jungle trees,
The misty wind of Eastern seas,
I am the bird who dreams today.
Tomorrow I'll fly far away.

—Abigail Purser

I felt sad listening to Abigail's poem. Her life had been cut short. She never got to go for her dreams. Never got to live a life past age eleven.

I opened my notebook and copied everything—Abigail's poem, the letter from her dad and the family tree.

We carefully placed the letters, the yellow ribbon with the tiny key on it, and the stationery back inside the small box. I shut the lid and locked it, leaving everything the way I'd found it.

As Toni closed the cardboard box, I stared at Abigail's name where I'd written it on my notebook. That was where she ended. She never had kids. Never got to see the world. Never did anything but dream about the life she would never have.

I sighed as a giggly little boy at the next table flicked paint at me.

Looked like I wasn't the first girl who wanted to get out of Abbington.

Ghost Seen in Graveyard; Hoax Suspected!

"THERE'S NO WAY I'm hanging out at this cemetery past dark," Toni said as she snapped photos. "I can't even believe I let you talk me into coming back here."

After reading through her things, I felt like we owed Abigail a visit. And anyway we hadn't really finished decorating her grave on Sunday. Of course, Toni wouldn't let me forget *why* we hadn't finished.

"I was practically eaten alive by a zombie, and you make me come back here?" she whined. She held the camera in front of her face. *Snap, snap, snap*.

"The guy with the glove was only trying to scare you," I said. "And don't forget this is also for a good grade in social studies." I bit back the fact that she needed me to keep her grades from plunging lower than they already were.

"Like grades are ever worth it. Is my life worth an A?" Toni asked. She kept stopping to investigate the slightest sound. "Did you hear that?"

"Yeah, it was my foot crunching a twig, you fraidy cat," I said, stomping down on some dry leaves for effect. "Just keep working so we can get out of here."

I used my sweatshirt to wipe dirt off the girl etched on Abigail's headstone. I thought about her poem. I whispered to her grave that I would think of her when I was older and traveling around the world. I would make a toast to all the interesting people I was meeting and say, "This is for a girl named Abigail."

I was kneeling there, thinking about all the stuff she missed from dying so early, when I heard a strange sound.

"Toni?" I called. No answer.

I called louder. "*Toni*?" Still no answer.

I looked past the grave and through the trees. Oh no. I forgot. We had just set the clocks back. The sun was nearly gone. I shivered.

"TO-NIIIIIII!" I hollered as loud as I could.

Then I felt a hand on my shoulder.

"Oh, it's you," I breathed a sigh of relief when I saw her. "Why didn't you answer when I called?"

"Casey," Toni whispered so softly I could barely hear her. "We have to get out of here right now."

"Why?" I whispered back. "Are you okay?"

"I . . . I . . ." Toni couldn't talk. She was really scared. "Over there," she whispered, pointing to a tree by the fence.

There, under the swaying branches of the birch just outside the fence, was a light shadow. It looked like a silhouette of a girl. I could make out a skirt and poofy sleeves. But she was floating in the air, hovering under the tree.

Then we heard a moan. The faint echo of a cry. Like the girl floating under the tree was crying out.

"It's a ghost!" Toni gasped, squeezing my arm so tight it hurt. "What are we going to—"

Suddenly an intense beam blinded me. It was right on us, so bright that I couldn't see beyond it.

"Who's there?" I yelled. But we heard only moaning.

We started backing away from the grave, toward the gate. We were clutching each other, navigating between tombstones.

"Casey," Toni whispered. "I think it's following us!"

For a half second I felt a stab of courage. What

if I rushed the light and gave the ghost or zombie or whatever it was a full-body tackle? But then the moaning got louder. And louder. It sucked away my strength.

There was only one thing to do.

"Run, Toni! Run!" I barked, taking off toward the gate.

I never ran so fast in my life.

Zombie Patrol Arrests Girl Reporter!

"OH, CASEY! THE party is going to be super here!" Megan exclaimed as I ran up to her. "We can set up a—hey, what's wrong with you?"

"Out . . . of . . . breath," I gasped. I had just run all the way from the graveyard to the Purser Farm in about three seconds flat.

"You look like you saw a ghost," Megan joked.

Is the girl ironic, or what? "Where's Toni?" I asked, still panting.

Just then Toni emerged from behind the barn, out of breath, her hair flying in every direction.

"Casey, you owe me!" she said, bending over and putting her hands on her knees and panting. "Can we go home now, please?"

"Did something happen at the cemetery?" Megan asked.

I shook my head. "No—"

"Yes!" Toni shrieked. "It was awful!"

Megan's mother joined us, her face tense with concern. "Are you girls okay? What happened?"

"You are never going to believe this," Toni began, "but we . . ."

I squeezed my eyes shut. And I'd thought I could keep the "haunting" rumors under control? Get real, Casey.

When I got home, I went straight to my room to e-mail Griffin. Tomorrow he was rolling in from Europe with his parents, and I wanted him to know everything. Especially the stuff from tonight. I sent off the e-mail, then realized I'd forgotten to tell him everything that had happened tonight. Duh.

To: Thebeast
From: Wordpainter

Sorry, dude. My longest e-mail ever! Okay, so I told you that Megan had to hear the whole story. And after that, her mom just wouldn't let it go.

Mrs. O'Connor was so upset that she grabbed a flashlight and her cell phone

and made us follow her back into that cemetery!

I admit I was afraid. But I also sort of wanted to go back with an adult and check out the ghost girl.

But you know what? When we got there it was quiet as a graveyard. No ghost. No light. Nada! There wasn't even an old vine or rope swing or anything at that tree. Did I feel stupid or what? E-ya soon.

After I clicked on Send, I turned off my computer and got ready for bed. I was tired and cold, "chilled to the bone," as my mom says. Even a hot shower didn't warm me up. Huddled under the covers in the dark, I tried to separate fact from fiction.

I couldn't stop thinking about that floating girl from the graveyard. The image just kept floating in my head. Haunting me. Pun intended.

Call me crazy, but I kept wondering if it was Abigail.

Did she know I had chosen her from all the other graves in Purser?

Did she know how much we had in common?

Had she come back to tell me something? To give me an important message?

I clicked on the bedside lamp and scribbled on the tiny notepad.

NOTE TO SELF: Have head
examined first thing tomorrow.

At least my head felt clear in the morning. I mean, a floating ghost girl? It was probably just a stuffed doll on a stick or something. Of course, once I landed at school I had to face a whole new barrage from the zombie patrol. To be honest, I was getting sick of being Trumbull's connection to the netherworld.

During my free period I ducked into the media center to escape my morbid fans. That's when I heard Madame Squeaky.

"Casey! Over here!" Megan called, waving like a tourist.

I sidled over to where Megan and Gary had spread their stuff out on a table. "Are you okay?" Megan asked. "After last night, I thought maybe—"

"I'm fine," I said through clenched teeth. "Ask me if the ghost slimed me and I'll give you a wedgie, I swear."

"Someone's in a bad mood," Gary said without looking up.

I could see that Megan and Gary were finishing their report on Gary's ancestors. My part was over. I had finished inputting our report at lunchtime. The only part left was the worst part—presentation. Luckily, Toni was doing it.

"Almost done?" I asked, dropping my stuff on the chair next to Gary's.

"We're just short one body and a few records," he said, flipping his pencil and catching it. "We still can't find anything on my great-great-grand-father."

"The librarian says kids have most likely lost the documents," Megan said. "And my dad hasn't been able to talk to his friend at the Historical Society."

"Boy, this dead guy sure is giving you a lot of grief," I said.

Gary frowned at my bad joke. "We had to shift the focus to my great-grandmother instead. Turns out she sold this awesome fudge that she made in her kitchen. After a couple of years, she had three factories."

"Go, grandma," I said. Then I thought about Gram. I was glad that she was a reporter. There were the obvious perks of having free fudge at your fingertips, but all that chocolate would eventually sizzle my circuits.

I was planning on getting some homework done. But then kids starting coming in to talk to me. The zombie patrol wanted the scoop on the latest, iratest ghost.

After the third interruption, I decided to take advantage of the situation. I interviewed every last person who bugged me about Purser. I wrote down so many quotes for my story that my hand was cramping.

DATELINE: Wednesday, October 28
SUBJECT: The Purser Project

Debbie Sitler: "I was planting some purple flowers when I saw the head of a statue turn and look right at me!"

Mike Brigman: "There were all these strange moaning noises. At first I thought it was my stomach 'cuz I traded for two Twinkies at lunch, but then it got louder and louder."

Shelly Amoroso: "A bright light chased me out of there before I finished cleaning the grave. I hope I can still get an A."

Stephanie Richardson: "I saw like, this

floating ghost? You know. She wore a dress and she was, like, moaning. But I didn't see much. 'Cause I just . . . I sort of ran like crazy. I was outta there, you know?"

Other kids had similar stories of the mysterious haunting at Purser. And their stories matched mine and Toni's word for word. Moan for moan.

I rubbed my nose. It was itching so much, you'd think it was stuck in a bag of pepper.

Was the cemetery really haunted with the ghost of Abigail Purser? Or was this whole thing just one big hoax?

I took my notebook and went off to hide in a carrel. Enough with being bugged by other students. Something about my Purser story was bugging me.

I thought about the times I'd gone by there before Halloween, before our school project. Just last summer I'd been to the farm with my parents to pick peaches. Mom and I had hiked through the graveyard without hearing the tiniest "Boo!" And last winter I'd been sledding on the hills there with my brother, Billy. No ghosts. No zombies. Not even an Abominable Snowman.

I scribbled in my notebook:

Why so many sightings? And why <u>now</u>?

A kid passing by with a poster-board covered with a family tree gave me the answer.

Because Purser Cemetery is filled with kids now.

6th graders

Perfect scare targets.

I bit my lower lip. There's nothing like an audience to bring out the ghosts.

CHAPTER 19

Velez Wins Hearts and Wows Crowds!

"AREN'T YOU NERVOUS?" I asked Toni. Not that I wanted to make her nervous. But it was Thursday afternoon, and we were next on the list to present our Day of the Dead project. Although Toni was doing the presentation, there were beads of sweat on my forehead.

"Just give me the report, Casey," Toni whispered. "Why are you sweating?"

"Sympathy sweat, I guess."

Toni smiled at me as she took the stack of papers—our report on Abigail. "I got you covered. Sit tight and watch Velez take center stage."

Ms. Hinkel called her up. The moment of reckoning had come.

"This is the story of Abigail Williams, who died when she was just eleven," Toni began.

"Casey and I don't have any relatives buried in Purser, but we chose Abigail because she was our age when she died. There wasn't any information on her in the library, but we tracked down a woman who . . ."

Toni was totally amazing.

She spoke in front of the class like it was the most natural thing in the world. Without looking at her notes, she covered all the important points in the report. She never missed a beat. Never choked. Never froze the way I do when my brain zones out. Did I mention that I hate talking to audiences?

Every few seconds she would stop to show the class some of the pictures she had taken. Each photograph was mounted on a piece of black cardboard, so it looked framed.

I was seriously impressed.

When she sat down, Toni looked over at me and stroked off an invisible point in the air.

Stupid? I don't think so.

I wanted to hug her. As a team, we had nailed the A. I was sure of it. And the pictures she used for the report would be perfect for my *Real News* story. I gushed after class. Yes, I, Casey Smith, gushed.

"All right, all right, Casey," Toni said, holding up a hand. "Don't get all mushy on me."

"Yeah, but—"

"Toni! Major score!" Gary called out, joining us. "I'm sure you aced it."

"Yeah, you rocked," Ringo said, high-fiving Toni.

I wanted to jump in and remind them both who wrote the report. But then I decided not to be such a limelight hog. For once.

"Toni was great," I agreed. "So were you." I pinged Ringo's arm. He and Tyler had presented their project yesterday, and who knew that an old river-mill could be so interesting? Of course, it helped that they tied in Old Man McKenzie's work with the Underground Railroad.

Gary lifted his baseball cap to scratch his head. "Man, I wish I was done with mine, too."

"Hey, zombie girls," someone called.

Toni and I turned together. Do you see how the zombie patrol was getting to us?

Jesse Moskowitz and Tim Carson were cruising over in their big droopy pants and big goofy grins.

"You two are so lucky," Tim said. "You got to do someone really cool."

"Yeah," I said, eyeing them curiously. Not that I didn't think Abigail was the perfect choice. But these pumpkin-heads could have picked her, too.

Jesse turned to Ringo, telling him: "And you stepped into a stink bomb, dude."

"No way." Ringo looked down at his sandals and red socks. "But I washed them yesterday. Is there anything more embarrassing than a bad smell?"

"Not your feet," Tim said, scowling at Ringo. "Your project. That slave lover. You forgot to point out that every time he gave some ex-slave a job, he was taking work from a decent white guy."

I couldn't believe what I was hearing. Was this another lame example of stupid middle-school boy humor? I looked over at Gary. He wasn't laughing.

None of us were.

Ringo's gray eyes lit up with anger as he stared down Tim. Ringo may be loopy, but sometimes he orbits back to earth. "That smell isn't my feet," he said quietly. "It's you. Racism reeks."

Tim's mouth twisted in a sick little smile. "Say what you want. But you can't tell me *they're* like *us*." He nodded toward Gary. "You can dress them in cool clothes, but they're still rejects."

"Are you crazy!" I almost spat at Tim.

My stomach tightened as I glanced at Gary. It hurt me that he was hearing this stuff. It hurt me that he was being hurt.

"Cut it out, Tim," I said. "So what if his skin's

a different color? *So what?* Do you hear what you're saying? It's like me telling you you're an idiot because you have green eyes." My hands balled into fists. My temper was rising. "You may be an idiot, but not because of your eye color, *Tim*.

Jesse snickered. "Whatever."

"Excuse me?" Toni stepped between me and the boys. "I wish I had a squeegee, 'cause I would run it right over both of your faces. Did you forget to take the trash out? Or does garbage always pour out of your mouths?" Her bracelets jingled as she wagged a finger at them.

Suddenly the two boys sank into themselves like two turtles going into their shells.

"Who do you think you are, attacking people like that?" Toni continued. "Passing judgment because someone's skin is different from your pasty butts?" She was talking so fast and furious that tiny balls of spit were showering Tim. "You want to see embarrassing? I'll show you embarrassing. Embarrassing is when your photo shows up in next week's paper with the caption 'Barf Mouth of the Week' underneath!"

"Dang, fine," Tim said. "Let's bail, Jesse James."

In a snap, they were gone. But Toni was still going.

"I can't believe how stupid people can be!"

she fumed. "Totally racist. Totally rude. Totally hurtful."

"I don't get it," I said, sneering after them. "They must have brains the size of fruit flies. Fly-brains!"

"Hel-lo?" Gary said. "Do we have to get into more name-calling here?"

I was surprised. "But, Gary, aren't you mad? You heard what they said."

"Sure, I'm mad. But I don't need you starting a war. And they don't rattle my cage. I am what I am—black and proud of it."

"Yeah," Ringo said. "They tried to rattle my cage, too. Back when I was trying out for the cheerleading squad those dudes were right on me. I guess they're just perennial rattlers. Like snakes."

"Snakes," I said thoughtfully. Sometimes Ringo's skewed logic was on target. "Poisonous snakes."

That afternoon, at the *Real News* meeting, Megan actually put aside party planning to focus on the paper. Clipboard in hand, she went over her checklist of what we needed for this week's edition. "Ringo, I don't think we've chosen a cartoon yet."

He sifted through a stack from the back of his notebook and handed her one. "This is one of my faves."

I peered over at Ringo's cartoon.

"Now that is one scary costume."

"Good." Megan nodded her approval. "And Casey, what's happening with your dyslexia story?" she asked.

"Well," I started. "I've got tons of info from the web. I e-mailed this doctor, but haven't heard back. And I—"

"She's going to interview me, so it doesn't have to be an editorial," Toni said, shocking me out of my sneakers.

"Are you serious?" I asked her.

"Yeah, I am, girl." She lifted her head, and her ponytail swung back like a fountain. "I don't care what kids think. Or say. I decided in the hall today that the truth is the coolest way to deal. Listening to Tim mouth off, I realized that I was hiding behind being different."

Gary looked up. "*You?* Hiding?"

Toni nodded. "But now I figure I gotta make this work for me. If I'm Mexican-American and dyslexic and a hottie—that's what I am. Let's blindside 'em with the real story."

Could something good have actually come from those manure mouths in the hall? Hard to believe.

For the second time that day I wanted to hug Toni. Jeez, was I going soft like Megan?

Then again, it was only one story. And I was slated to have two running in the next issue. Once again, my front-page story wasn't all the way there. Dang!

"Casey, I had an idea about your graveyard piece," Megan said, as if she could read my thoughts. "How about if we run the graveyard story with the interviews you have, and leave it a mystery? Sort of like a special Halloween thriller."

"Tell me you're joking," I said, mousing

around on the computer. Griffin was supposed to be back, but so far he hadn't e-mailed me.

"Or," she went on, "we could run it in the next issue, after you've solved the mystery."

I wished I could bat her away like a fly. Pesky, perky Megan. "Megan, a haunted graveyard story has to run before Halloween weekend—or not at all," I said. "Timing is key in journalism."

"Thanks for telling me something I already know," she said. We have these little showdowns. It's fine. Even though I sometimes kick myself for voting for her for editor-in-chief. What was I thinking?

"So what do you need to finish the story, Casey?" Megan said. Was that annoyance in her voice? At *moi*?

"I want to know who's haunting the graveyard," I said. "I don't buy this whole floating girl, zombie business. Not after being around that cemetery dozens of times in the past few years and not seeing a thing. I think someone is staging pranks because they know sixth graders are visiting the place now."

"Interesting theory," Megan said, lifting her pencil, pink with glitter hearts. "But how can you prove it?"

"A stakeout," I said. "I have a plan to trap the culprit. But I need help. Today."

"Whoa. You're going to hide and wait for the haunters?" Gary asked.

"Just like a commando mission," Ringo added. "Melody could make the dog tags. She's good with metal."

Toni remained silent. She'd warned me—no more graveyards. But she watched us intently as she unwrapped a fruity-smelling piece of bubble gum.

"It's too dangerous," Megan said. "It's totally crazy."

"Halloween is crazy turned inside out," Ringo said, scratching his purple head. "Count me in."

"Yeah, me too," Gary said, high-fiving Ringo.

"Wait," Megan said. "What parent in her right mind will drive us to a graveyard? Especially after everything that's been going on at Purser?"

"My gram," I said, turning to the guys to start making a plan.

"Wait," she said again. "Casey, you keep ignoring the fact that this could be dangerous."

"Megan," I said through clenched teeth. "Sometimes you need to get out of your cushy editor's chair if you want a story that—"

"Hold up, Casey," Toni interrupted me. "Don't go getting your jeans in a wad. Listen Megan, there's safety in numbers. It's a good plan. I vote we do it."

"You're in?" I asked, blown away. She swore she'd never go back there. And at night? This was a shocker.

"I'm in, girl," Toni said, smacking her gum.

We all turned to Megan.

She looked around. She bit her lip. She fiddled with the pink lace on the cuffs of her sweater.

Finally, she asked, "What time will you be picking me up?"

Alien and Cyclops Spotted in Purser Cemetery!

I HATE TO bug Gram while she's writing. Genius shouldn't be interrupted.

So on that Thursday, after school, I stood at her closed door for five minutes and listened as she typed. When I heard the tap-tap of the keys stop, I would knock. Lightly.

Just my luck, Gram was on a roll. Her nails clicked on the keyboard like a Broadway dancer.

"Uh, Gram?" I finally called through the door. I felt like a five-year-old who had just broken a lamp. No response. I knocked. "Gram? It's Casey." Not that the First Lady of the United States would be in our house and bothering Gram on a Thursday afternoon.

The door opened. Gram was in her red silk kimono, her working duds.

"You rang?" she said in her best stodgy butler voice.

"Am I interrupting?" I asked, biting a nail.

"Yes, of course," Gram said, raising an eyebrow. "But what can I do you for?"

"I need a favor," I said, sticking my hands in the pockets of my jeans as far as they would go. "I need a ride. To Purser. I need to catch a rat. The gray-glove boy. I think he's just some kid who's staging all the haunted things that go bump over there."

Gram folded her arms.

"And exactly how do you plan on catching this one-gloved mystery person?" she asked.

"Well, a bunch of us are going to hide there and wait," I said. "It's a stakeout. We're going to bust the little booger!"

Gram rubbed her forehead. Bad sign. She only rubs her forehead when she's writing and can't come up with the right words to say what she wants to say.

"Listen, Casey," she said slowly. "I'm not so sold on the idea of taking a car full of eleven-year-olds to a cemetery. Especially if there really is someone there. I don't fancy having four sets of parents yelling at me that I put their kids in danger."

"Gram, you said you trusted me," I whined.

Not something I do a lot of.

"I can't believe you're pulling the trust card on me," Gram said, scratching her head and making her short mussy hair more mussy. She stared at me for a long minute. I thought for sure I was shut down.

"Do I get to wear dark clothes and carry a flashlight?" she asked.

"Uh, yeah—sure!"

She nodded. "Then it's a deal." She clicked on Save on the computer. "If we're going on a stakeout, how about some cheese steak subs to get us in the mood?"

"Great!" I nearly yelped as I raced out of her room.

How lucky am I to have Gram as my gram?

I ran to the phone to set things in motion. I called Toni, who would call Ringo and Gary. Then Gary would call Megan. Ringo would call Melody. I'd asked Tyler to come along, but he had an English paper due tomorrow. Toni was impressed that Gram was providing door-to-door service. So was I. I'd sort of bluffed when I'd told Megan that Gram was a sure thing.

After I hung up, I bolted to the garage to get some gear. I grabbed two flashlights, checked their batteries and dumped them in my backpack. Then I went upstairs and changed into a dark brown T-shirt and my brown sneakers. I already had on black jeans. When I looked in the mirror and saw my outfit with my brown eyes, brown hair and light brown freckles, I thought I looked like one big mudslide.

By the time we'd grabbed dinner and picked up the crew, I was psyched. What would my parents say if they knew I was spending the evening in a graveyard with my grandmother and five other kids?

Good thing they were thousands of miles away.

Since there was no parking by the graveyard, Gram pulled into Purser's dusty lot, and we spilled out of the Jeep.

"I feel a bit like I'm in a movie," Melody said, adjusting her backpack.

"It's cold out here!" Megan whined, rubbing her hands. Was she really wearing a powder-blue jacket with fake fur to a stakeout?

"Special-assignment agent Ringo reporting for duty!" Ringo said, doing some karate moves. Then he saluted Gary. "Agents, gather 'round. I have gear for the commando mission."

We followed him to the back of Gram's Jeep. Ringo opened the duffel bag he'd stowed there, and out spilled Martian antennae and masks and bulging eyes and hats.

"Whoa. Did you raid the drama department?" Gary asked. He put on a pair of big glasses with fat eyeballs on long springs.

I bit back a laugh. "Okay, can you tell me why we're doing this?"

Ringo stuck his pointy ears on and completed the look with a pair of fake fangs. "I figure, if we're a little scary looking, maybe we won't be so scared."

That's Ringo logic.

Gram strapped on a pair of green, glittery antennae.

Ringo handed Megan a mask. "But it's . . . it's ugly," she complained.

"That's the point!" Toni said, slipping on a monster mask that covered her eyes and nose and made her look positively evil.

Melody wore a big green wig and red nose.

I was forced into wearing a pair of those glasses with the big fake nose and mustache. I thought, Now I'm a Super Nerd mudslide. This was not my kind of makeover.

We started walking in the direction of the cemetery. It had just gotten dark, so the booths and pumpkin patch were still cranking with kids and their parents. We passed one worker guy who was dressed in one of those black outfits with human bones painted on.

"Looks like they've got the *skeleton* crew working tonight," Gary said. I punched his arm. "Just a joke! Dang!"

We hiked outside the festival grounds and started up the path to the cemetery.

"Shall we dig a hole and cover it with leaves?" Melody asked, with a giggle. "Like a tiger trap for a zombie?"

"Definitely!" Gary said. "Or one of those rope-pulley things in a tree that yanks the bad guy up in the air when he steps in it! We can leave zombie dude hanging all night!"

Everyone started giggling and throwing in ridiculous television ideas. Everyone but me, that is. I was getting ants in my pants. This haunting was a big deal. Someone had to be up to something. But everyone else acted like we were going apple-bobbing.

"Can you guys just chill?" I said in a controlled voice. "You're going to blow it."

I was going to get this story if it was the last thing I ever did.

And I hoped finding out it really was a fake haunting was *not* the last thing I ever would do.

We gathered at the entrance of the cemetery. I gave everyone their stakeout positions.

Gary and Toni hid just inside the gate, by the moving angel statue. Megan, Melody and Gram took the center section. Ringo was with me by the back corner, next to Abigail's grave. If someone popped out of the hole near the fence, we were in the perfect position to catch them.

At last, we were in place. In the darkness, the rows of tombstones barely stood out against the deep purple sky. I shivered, but not from the cold.

Silence. Then I heard Gram giggling with the girls.

"Everyone!" I called in a loud whisper. "Ssshhhhh!"

Two minutes later I could still hear Gram. And there was no mistaking Megan's squeal. "Gram, Megan! Zip it!" I called. Gram was having so much fun, she was going to ruin the stakeout.

It seemed like we waited there forever. But Ringo had a watch that lit up in the dark when he pushed a button. Twenty minutes on a stakeout sure does feel like two hours.

I sagged against Abigail's cold gravestone. I ran my fingers over the etched girl. Even though she lived a hundred years before me, I felt like we were like each other in so many ways. She loved books. She loved to write. She wanted to travel. Would all that be on Casey Smith's tombstone?

Ugh! I shivered.

"This is the grave where the girl in your report

is buried?" Ringo whispered. When I nodded, he added, "Abigail rocks."

"Yeah, she did," I whispered back. "I wish I could meet her now. Talk to her about . . . stuff."

"Maybe you could find a psychic at a carnival or something!" Ringo's whisper was getting louder. "And Abigail could enter her body and you could talk to her and tell her about *Real News*."

"Oh right, like I'd really tell a girl who's been dead a hundred years about Trumbull Middle School!" I said, realizing that I was actually having a conversation about speaking to a dead girl through a carnival psychic. "Ringo, of all the wack-a-doo stuff you—"

Then I heard something. Like leaves under a boot. My heart started to pound. "Ringo? Did you—"

"Yeah, I heard it," he whispered.

Without breathing I stood up and started moving away from Abigail's grave. Slowly. One step at a time. Quietly.

I was watching Ringo move around Abigail's tombstone, when *thump!* I bumped into something. I reached behind me and felt . . . what? Cloth? A skirt? A sleeve? Was it a body?

I spun around. And I was face-to-face with a girl hanging from a tree.

Journalist Trapped in Body of Eleven-Year-Old Girl!

I BOLTED OVER to Ringo, on the other side of Abigail's grave. My heart was hammering through my chest. It's not real, it's not real, it's not real! I said to myself over and over again.

"Ringo, it has to be stuffed, " I whispered, trying to convince him and myself at the same time.

Ringo was freaked, but trying to deal. "Stuffed?" he asked, wiping his upper lip. Then he calmed down a little and stood up to look. "Wait, I'm with you. Who would wear a ruffled shirt with a wrap skirt? Major clashing action happening, dudette."

I yanked on his sleeve, and we hunkered down by the gravestone. "I wish I had a camera."

"Me, too." Ringo nodded. "I'd love a video-camera. Or maybe one of those Polaroid things."

"Shhh," I whispered, "the haunter must be nearby."

I could hear myself breathing. Ringo's nose started to whistle, and he didn't do anything about it. I reached over and pinched it.

Then we heard footsteps. Leaves crunching under footsteps, actually.

They came closer . . . closer . . . until the head of a one-eyed ogre appeared around Abigail's grave. Megan.

"You scared my fangs off!" Ringo said.

"Sorry," she whispered. "I wanted to see what was going on, so I ditched your gram and Melody and sneaked over."

"Get down here!" I ordered, pulling Megan down by her ridiculous jacket. "The haunter is here! Don't say a word!"

We heard more leaves underfoot. Then we heard that freaky moaning, the same sad crying I had heard with Toni. The hair rose on my arms.

Ringo moved back a little to give Megan room to crouch down behind the gravestone. He slipped and accidentally unearthed a big clump of leaves.

"Tell me that leaf-crunching isn't Gary coming to check on me," I said.

"No," Ringo said, "I just uncovered some

insects and it's . . . Yo, yikes!" Ringo leaped up. "Sorry, bug dudes." He'd almost fallen and smashed the freshly unearthed community of creepy crawlers.

Suddenly, a blinding beam of light swung our way.

I glanced up.

Just as Ringo's fanged face was caught in a sheet of white light.

CHAPTER
22

Sherlock Homies
Crack Case!

"NOW!" I SHOUTED, jumping to my feet. "Everyone! Go!"

The cemetery was a light show of flashlights. Everyone jumped up from their positions and turned their flashlights toward the bright light. Shadows of gothic grave markers danced as our light beams swung around.

"Go! Go! Go!" I hollered, high-stepping through leaves and tombstones and flowers toward the light. Within seconds we closed in, forming a semicircle.

We slowed, moving toward the light like a drill team of Halloween freaks: Super Nerd, Chuckles the Clown, Fang Boy, Ogre Girl, Evil Antoinette, Eyeball Boy and Alien Grandma.

169

"Don't stop!" I shouted as we closed in on the light.

"Safety in numbers!" Megan called. "Safety in numbers!"

"All right!" I yelled. "Whoever you are, you're busted!"

The light went out. We stopped.

"Get out of town!" Gary suddenly hollered. "Brandon! What're you doing here?"

Brandon was Gary's older brother. He was in high school. And he wasn't alone. There were three other guys from Abbington High School. They were all dressed in dark clothes and had smudges on their faces. And they were laughing hysterically.

"Gary, does Mom know you're here after dark?" Brandon asked, stepping out from behind a double tombstone.

"I can't believe my own brother is the guy who's been haunting Purser Cemetery," Gary said.

"Well, live with it, little brother." Brandon turned to his friends. "Come on, guys. It's over."

One of the guys hoisted up a big spotlight like the ones in the Trumbull drama department. Another kid had a big boom box. That explained the blinding light and creepy noises.

And one guy was wearing a tattered gray glove!

"You!" I said, marching over to a boy who was about two feet taller than me. Okay, I was a little intimidated, but I was on a roll. "You're the hand in the hole! Who do you think you are, scaring kids like that?"

He just laughed at me. "Hold up, my little Sherlock Homie," he said, removing the glove and sticking it in his back pocket. "It's not like I hurt anybody."

"Tell me how you did it, and maybe I'll show you some mercy," I ordered. They all looked at each other and laughed so hard, you'd think I just told them I was a supermodel.

"Mercy?" Brandon said. "What exactly do you think you can—"

"She can report you to the police," Gram interrupted, stepping forward. Her antennae bobbed, but she still packed a wallop. When the boys saw Gram, they choked up. Nothing like a little adult supervision.

Then I got some answers.

It was all Brandon's idea. And these guys claimed they weren't doing anything wrong. They found a way to string up the angel statue with a vine so they could make it spin around. They found a place to scare kids through the fence, then get away through the tunnel. They figured out how to rig up a stuffed dummy girl to make it look like a floating ghost.

They did it all.

Gary was Brandon's tip-off that sixth graders were going to be at Purser, working on their projects.

"You boys should be ashamed of yourselves," Gram said. "You could have hurt someone. I wonder what your parents and the police would think of all this."

Now the guys stared at the ground. All except Brandon. "You can't have us arrested." He stared right at Gram, his face as cold as stone.

She gave him the Gram glare, antennae and all. "For the moment, I'll be satisfied with turning you over to the manager at Purser Farms. They own the graveyard. If they want to have you make amends, you might be spending more time in this cemetery than you planned."

When Gram was done helping them get in touch with their consciences, we all headed back to Purser Farms.

I walked at the front of the pack, near Gary and Brandon.

"What's with you?" Gary asked his brother. "You rigged up pranks in the cemetery, scared my friends, who knows what else. What is *with* you?"

Brandon shook his head. "Are you dense? It was just for fun. Harmless fun to scare some brats out of the graveyard. Who really cares? Ease up, bro."

"I care! I've had it with you," Gary said.

After that, they were silent all the way back to the farm. The festival was winding down for the night, but Gram managed to find a manager, who took the situation pretty seriously. He gave Brandon and his friends a stern lecture. Then he made them sit on a bale of hay until their parents could get there to pick them up.

While the stakeout crew was piling back into Gram's Jeep, I looked back toward the cemetery. My news nose wasn't twitching, but I had a funny feeling.

Something more than a bunch of dumb kids pulling pranks was going on here. But what?

Girl Reporter Digs Up Goofus Ghouls!

FRIDAY MORNING. I was sitting in the *Real News* office polishing my story when Gary cruised in. He leaned over my shoulder and read my awesome headline:

HAUNTED CEMETERY: GHOUL REPORTER DIGS UP REAL GHOULS!

I reached around and patted myself on the back. Nothing starts a day off better than a front-page story. Have I mentioned that?

"Not bad, Casey," he said, slumping into a chair. "Glad I could help."

I stopped typing. Suddenly I was sitting with Mr. Sincerity. Not that it bothered me to lap up some praise. But Gary was not one to give it out. Something was wrong.

"Gary, you okay?" I asked.

"No, I'm not okay," he said theatrically. Then he grabbed a rubber minifootball from his backpack and started tossing it in the air and catching it. Over and over again.

I sat down across the table from him. "Spill."

"Spill what?" Gary asked.

"What happened last night when your parents found out what Brandon was doing in the cemetery?" I asked. I mean, duh.

"Oh, *that*," he said, looking at the football like it stunk. "My mom was furious. Brandon hates me now. But that's okay, since I sort of hate him back. My dad called me a tattletale. My mom yelled at my dad. They apologized when they found out the whole truth. But it was basically a bad scene all around."

"Jeez, sorry, Gary," I said. Who would have thought that solving the graveyard mystery would cause major fireworks at Gary's house?

"And that's not even the half of it," he added. "I knew Brandon wasn't telling me something. I just had a feeling there was more going on there than just my big bro having a good laugh at scared sixth graders."

So Gary had a feeling too, huh?

"You know, Gary," I said, "I had a feeling that something else was up."

"Well, you were right," Gary said, throwing the football as hard as he could against the wall. "There was something at Purser that Brandon didn't want me—or any of the other kids—to find out about. Brandon staged that haunting to keep me from finding out a family secret."

"What?" I asked, trying not to look too eager.

"What what?" Gary asked, pretending not to be upset.

"What was Brandon trying to hide?" I asked slowly. Double duh.

Gary sighed. "You sure you want to know?" he asked.

"Is a frog's butt watertight?" I responded.

Gary actually smiled.

Then he started talking. "I couldn't find Jacob Williams's grave because I was looking in the wrong part of the cemetery. Jacob was a white man." He explained that Brandon had the same Day of the Dead assignment when he was in middle school. Clean a grave, look up your ancestry. But when Brandon looked up his family roots, he learned that his (and Gary's) great-great-grandfather was Jacob Williams, a white man. That meant that Brandon—and Gary—had a white ancestor. Brandon was upset to learn he was related to a white man. So upset, he decided he never wanted anyone else to find out.

"So he destroyed the family Bible and trashed the three files from the library that told the story of Jacob Williams and my great-great-grandmother, Sarah Taylor," Gary said.

"Wow. So I guess your Jacob was related to Abigail," I said.

He nodded. "I checked it out. They were cousins."

"Why didn't your parents tell you?" I asked.

"Brandon never told them. My mother was pretty surprised by all this, too. My dad remembers talk of a white ancestor when he was a kid, but back then, when he asked, he parents wouldn't talk about it. I guess families keep some things secret." He crossed the room to get his football.

I watched him slump back into a chair and fiddle with the football. He looked so hurt that I wished I had secret powers so I could make a cheer-him-up ice-cream sundae magically appear. Still, I couldn't tell if he was bummed because of Brandon, or because he had discovered that he had a white ancestor. Gary had always celebrated being black. He was proud of his race and his heritage like no one I knew. Did Jacob Williams change all that?

"Gary," I said, knowing full well that now I was getting nosy. "Are you ashamed of your brother? Or your great-great-grandfather?"

Gary chucked the football against the wall again. "I know Brandon's ashamed," he finally said. "He hid the truth for a while. But when I came home and told him about my assignment, he must've lost it."

Uh, yeah. Just a little.

"I guess he was worried that I'd find a way to connect the family tree back to Jacob Williams," Gary continued. "He thought he was protecting himself by getting his friends to help him haunt the cemetery."

"As long as kids were afraid of the place, they'd stay away," I said. It was a bummer for Gary, for sure. But it was one killer front-page story. Of course, I didn't say that out loud. I have my sensitive moments. Swear.

Gary smacked the football from one hand to another. "All night long, I kept thinking of Sally Hemings. Pretty weird."

"Sally Hemings?" I frowned. "Who's she?"

"She was a slave in the late 1700s. Thomas Jefferson's slave." He picked up a computer print-out from the desk and skimmed it as he talked to me. "I read about her a while ago, but I just got more info from the web. Some historians say

Jefferson was the father of some of her children. Recently, they did some DNA testing to link Jefferson with Sally. The results show that he probably was the father of at least one of her children. But descendants of Sally Hemings made the connection years ago. They hold family reunions. They've even been fighting to be buried with the Jefferson family."

"So one of our presidents probably had kids with one of his slaves?" I shook my head. "Gee, I wonder why they never taught us *that* in second-grade history."

"It's even more twisted than that," Gary said. "The thing is, Jefferson had more than a hundred slaves, and he treated them as property. He thought Africans were inferior beings. So how did he treat Sally?"

"And did she have any choice?" "I said. "I mean, she was a slave."

"Exactly," Gary said, still palming the football.

"But Gary, Sarah wasn't a slave when she met Jacob Williams. I mean, they probably weren't allowed to get married, but some things were different from Jefferson's time."

"I know that," he said. "But it's all so weird. You think you know who you are, then you don't. Not really. Finding out that I have white blood . . . it really threw me."

"All blood is red, Gary," I said. Ugh. Was I that preachy?

"Whatever, Casey," Gary said, standing and yanking his backpack onto one shoulder. "It's still the blood of a white man. It chips away at who I thought I was. I was proud to be black. All black."

"And now?" I asked.

He headed to the door, picked up his football, then turned and looked right at me.

"Now I don't know."

Princess of Pink
Lost in Munchkinland!

JACK O'LANTERN   SIMON O'LANTERN

THERE'S NOTHING LIKE a Friday night to give a girl a case of the happies. A finished front-page story for Monday's paper was pretty thrilling, too.

I cruised upstairs and tossed my backpack

on my bed. Then I flipped on my computer. I tried to log on to the website the librarian had mentioned—Old Abbington. Bingo. For the first time, it came up in splendiferous gold and red, with a picture of the Massachusetts state flag in the corner. I typed in "Jacob Williams." Brandon had pilfered the files from the library, but he didn't have access to the copies at the Historical Society.

Jackpot.

There were a few pages on Jacob Williams, and on Sarah Taylor. The Old Abbington website was a treasure. Too bad it hadn't been up and running last week. I hit print and then clicked on my e-mail icon. I had a problem only Griffin could help me with.

To: Thebeast
From: Wordpainter

GRIF! In desperate need of costume. Party tonight at Purser Farms! Not keen on splattering ketchup on myself again this year. Not a fan of cutesy costumes, à la Megan "Sugarplum Fairy" O'Connor. Please advise!

Oh, P.S.: Cemetery haunting a total hoax.

Stupid high schoolers being all big and trying to scare the little sixth graders. And more. Will tell all later. But you can write and tell me how great I am now! HA!

I sat there for about a million minutes waiting for his reply. Finally, my computer bleeped. I read his suggestion for a costume and yelled, "Yes!" How obvious! It would be a brrrrilliant get-up!

For the next hour, I scrambled like a lunatic to pull a costume together. Gram was standing in the doorway to my bedroom, watching me unload my closet onto my floor.

"Gram, don't you have a safari vest or something that has tons of pockets?" I asked. "Something! Anything!"

"Are you supposed to be a tourist in Zimbabwe?" she asked.

"Very funny," I said, looking at myself in the mirror. "What do you think of this hat?"

"Very safari-ish," she said. "What's the costume?"

"Not safari!" I said, stomping my foot. "I'm supposed to be a foreign correspondent for CNN!"

"Oh, pardon me," she said, holding up a hand. "Let me go check my stuff."

Gram set me up with an old broken video-camera and a zippered vest with minibinoculars in one pocket. Then she made a microphone out of cardboard and foil and attached a long piece of black yarn for the cord. I already had cargo pants and the pith helmet, so I was good to go.

"Should I smudge my face?" I asked as we climbed into Gram's Jeep.

"Only if you're assigned to cover the Great Mud Wars of the Mawindi," she said, grinning at me.

On the way to Purser Farms, I told Gram about Brandon's big reason for haunting the graveyard. And I told her about how Gary was so shaken up about having a white ancestor. "Do you think I should tell him what I learned about Jacob Williams on the Internet tonight?" I asked.

"Ask him," she suggested. "People can have a strong sense of racial identity. Wouldn't it be a jolt to you to have held so tight to that identity your whole life, then suddenly learn that you're not exactly who you thought you were?"

"I guess you're right," I said. When isn't she?

As I was getting out of the Jeep at Purser, Gram handed me five bucks and told me to have fun. I plunked on my helmet and headed toward the party.

"Casey!" I heard a squeal. The squeal of none other than . . .

"Megan," I said, taking in her costume. "Did you follow the Yellow Brick Road?"

"Don't you love it?" she said, twirling around in her blue dress and ruby-red slippers. "My mom did my braids, and I came up with the idea to put a stuffed puppy in a basket! I just love *The Wizard of Oz*, don't you?"

"As much as the next girl, I'm sure," I said, looking over her shoulder to find someone I knew so I could ditch her.

"Thanks soooo much for suggesting Purser!" she squeaked. "It's perfect. I didn't have to decorate or anything!"

I am not kidding when I say that her voice was so high-pitched that I expected dogs from miles around to come running.

Catching a flash of movement from the corner of my eye, I jumped back as a guy in a hockey uniform skated up to me. He had brown skin, short cropped hair and a cute smile. Definitely familiar. But I couldn't place him.

"Easy there, Roller Boy," I said. "You almost sliced off my toes."

"Not even close, Case," he answered.

I blinked. "Gary? Nice costume."

I couldn't help but grin. And then, in a flash, he skated off toward a line of other skaters.

"Oh, look at that line for the in-line skating slalom course!" Megan said, nearly piercing my eardrum. "The obstacles are scarecrows, glowing jack-o'-lanterns and haystacks! Couldn't you just die!"

Yes. I could die. From an overload of Megan cheesiness. Please, someone, rescue me.

Suddenly—

"Rah!" growled an undead dude from behind a scarecrow. "Anybody thirsty?"

It was Spence Woodham, Megan's older-boy crush. I had to grin. Call me crazy, but he was a cute zombie. Megan could seriously bag the babes. Even though he scared her so bad, she nearly dropped her puppy.

"Oh, Spence!" she yelped. "You scared me so!"

Scared her so? So . . . what? I had to get out away from Dorothy the Dorkster.

"Casey!" I heard Ringo. "Get over here."

I cruised over toward Ringo and Melody, who were attached at the hip. Melody's hair was bright green. Ringo's was still bright purple. They both wore pointy ears, and they shared one huged tattered shirt. They had splattered fake blood all over the shirt and glued plastic bugs and worms everywhere.

Toni stood with them, looking so dramatic I thought she could be in a Broadway play. She was a tiger. How perfect.

"You look killer," I said. And was it my imagination, or was Toni in a good mood?

"Thanks, Casey," she said. "I'm stoked! Ms. Hinkel caught me after school today and told me that we aced our Day of the Dead report."

"Woohoo!" I high-fived her. "That rocks!"

"Rocks." Ringo turned to Melody and shook the material of her sleeve. "We should have glued on rocks and dirt. You know, make it look like we just scratched our way out of the grave."

Melody nodded. "Maybe next year, my dear zombie friend."

"Translation? What are you guys?" I asked.

"We're a two-headed, four-legged zombie, aren't we?" Melody singsonged. "Do you like it?"

"Cool," I said, secretly wondering how long it would take Melody to get that lime green out of her hair. "Hey, how about cruising with me over to the cemetery? I've got a finishing touch for Abigail's grave."

Toni gave me a tiger growl, and I held up my hands. "Okay, not you. I didn't mean you."

"Ringo, you go," Melody said. "I've got to go visit the loo."

"Lou who?" Ringo asked, turning his head and bumping his nose against Melody's nose.

Melody giggled and extracted herself from the costume. Ringo adjusted the giant shirt, and we set off down the trail to the graveyard.

Just as we left the light of the farm, I heard a rustle in the leaves behind us. I stopped and glared at a fat tree trunk. "All right," I said. "Whoever you are, you don't scare me!"

Tyler jumped out from behind a tree and hollered some cheesy he-man battle cry.

I tipped back my pith helmet. "Tyler, do you know how old this is getting? Give it a rest, already!"

He grabbed me, put his arm around my neck, knocked off my hat and started giving me a noogie.

"Hey! Stop!" I said. "That burns."

"It's supposed to," he said, letting me go. "Why are you guys all the way out here?"

"Why are *you* out here?" I asked. He made a killer vampire—pun intended. There was fake blood on his chin and everything. And I have to admit, my palms were still sweating from being grabbed by him, even if it *was* for a vampire noogie.

"I was following you," he said, flashing that

crooked grin. No fangs on this vamp. Just one adorable crooked tooth. I about melted.

"Come on," I said, starting toward the cemetery. "I have something I need to do."

Berlin Wall
Crumbles, Again!

WHEN WE GOT to the cemetery, I went straight to Abigail's grave. I reached in my pocket and pulled out my piece of Berlin Wall, the one my parents had gotten for me. Earlier, when I'd been getting dressed, I'd spotted it in my room and the realization hit me like like a chunk of concrete between the eyes. This was the perfect gift for Abigail.

I held it over her grave and wondered if she would know it was here. She always wanted to travel. I figured that something from a foreign city would be the perfect thing to leave her. I put it right between the candles and plastic flowers.

"Why are you giving Abigail a rock?" Ringo asked.

"It's a magic rock." I stood up and brushed

the dirt off the knees of my cargo pants. "Stare at it too long, and you'll turn into a grasshopper. Let's roll."

"Really?" Ringo closed one eye and peeked at it. "I wouldn't mind being turned into a millipede. All those arms remind me of the oars of a Viking ship."

"I was going to be a Viking," Tyler said as we headed toward the gate. "But I couldn't get one of those weird hats with horns in it."

It scared me a little that Tyler was beginning to tune in to Ringo's wavelength.

On our way out, we spotted Gary. He was standing in front of a grave in the white section of the cemetery. I had a feeling it was the grave of Jacob Williams.

"You guys go ahead, okay?" I said. "I'll catch up with you at the skating course."

I walked up behind Gary and stood there for a minute without saying anything. But that was about as long as I could go without opening my mouth. "You want to know some stuff about this guy?" I asked. "Because I did some research, and I know a fact or two."

Gary sighed. "Yeah. Whatever. Let's hear it."

"Jacob Williams. Well, your great-great-grandfather wanted to be an explorer, but he got stuck in Abbington running the family business," I said.

I felt like I was on the Biography Channel. "His dad got sick, so he had to take over, and that pretty much canceled any traveling plans. Jacob was married, but his wife died when he was in his thirties. A few years later, he met Sarah Taylor."

I stopped for a second to see if Gary was into it. His face didn't change much. So I just kept going. "Sarah was an artist," I said. "She painted portraits of African-Americans in the community. They never married. I think it might have been against the law back then for a black person to marry a white person. But they were together until they died."

"Getting married would have caused a scandal," Gary suggested.

"Definitely," I agreed. "But they did have a child. Sarah wanted to return to her hometown of Boston to raise the boy, but decided to stay in Abbington. She had a good business here. And she wanted to raise her son in the country. That son was your great-grandfather."

There was a long silence when I finished. Finally he turned to me.

"I've been trying to wish this whole thing away," he said. "But hearing that . . . I don't know. What would have happened if Sarah and Jacob had never met?"

"Or if she stayed in Boston that summer?" I added.

"Then I wouldn't be Gary," he said, squinting. "Trip out, huh?"

"Yeah." I studied the grave.

"I'd like to see the info you dug up," he said. "I'm thinking about doing my social studies project on Jacob now. Though Megan's going to tear her hair out if we don't get it done soon."

I swallowed. "Megan isn't the problem, Gary. It's people like Tim and Jesse. If you do your project on Jacob, everyone in school is going to know about your ancestry. I mean, are you ready to flash your family tree, bare and naked?"

He shrugged. "Maybe I shouldn't. But maybe I should. What was it Toni said? Blindside 'em with the truth."

The wind kicked up, blowing leaves past our feet. The cemetery didn't seem scary anymore. Actually, with all the new flowers and paper decorations, it reminded me of a giant birthday cake.

And standing there on that giant birthday cake, I didn't know what to tell Gary. Which is rare for Casey Smith, girl reporter with strong opinions.

"Well," I finally said, "whatever you decide, it'll be right. The thing is, I'll stand by you whether you're related to Jacob or Jehoshaphat Williams."

"Who's that?"

I grinned. "I just like to say the name. Jehoshaphat."

Gary laughed. "Maybe having a white ancestor isn't so terrible. I'm that much more different now."

"Like, how?"

"How many kids at Trumbull are just like me?" He lifted his chin and pointed at his chest with his thumb. "None! That's how many. I stand alone."

"Yeah," I said. "You totally stand out." He always has.

Gary high-fived me.

"Absolutely, Casey Smith," he said, reaching down and clearing away a stray weed from Jacob's grave. "I'm Jacob William's great-great-grandson. Is that a mindwarp, or what?"

It was. But I was already getting used to it. "You want to know something else, Gary?" I asked, scratching under my pith helmet.

"Sure, what?"

"I'm sick of this graveyard. Let's bail."

"Amen to that," Gary said.

As we turned to go I noticed another girl in the cemetery. She was in a costume—a fancy yellow dress with lots of ruffles and a puffy petticoat.

She also wore a huge yellow hat with lots of bows on it, and there was a yellow ribbon tied in a bow around her neck. Talk about a serious costume.

"Hey! You going back to the party?" Gary called across the tombstones.

She walked toward us, her long brown curls bouncing a little with each step.

"It's a big party, isn't it?" she said, looking at me.

"Sure it is," I said. "Dorothy from Kansas put it on. It has to be a big deal."

"Dorothy from Kansas?" she asked.

"Just a puffball princess who happens to be the school's number one organizer," I said. I sort of appreciated Megan's efforts. I couldn't throw a party like this, even though I'd never admit that to anyone.

"We were just heading back," Gary said. "Cruise with us."

"Oh, I have to stay here," she said, looking at my homemade microphone. "What's that?"

"This?" I held it up. "It's my microphone for interviewing foreign delegates. I'm supposed to be a reporter overseas."

"Oh, I see. How thrilling for you," she said, staring at me with big brown eyes.

"We'll be at the skating course when you're done cleaning your grave," Gary said. "Come find us."

She smiled. Her teeth were sort of crooked.

"Yeah, come find us," I said. "What's your name?"

"Abby," she said, touching a curl.

"Cool. See you later," I said. Then we turned toward the gate and started back to the farm.

Just as we reached the fence, a thought stopped me dead in my tracks. Abby? Short for Abigail?

I spun around. The girl was gone. Vanished. Could that have been—? Did we just—?

"What?" Gary asked, watching me look around like I'd just lost my keys.

"Where'd that girl go?" I asked.

Gary turned back and folded his arms over his hockey jersey. "She's probably behind a tomb, cleaning some grave."

I didn't mention to Gary that I'd never seen that girl around. Or that she was wearing a yellow ribbon around her neck, very much like the one I'd found in Abigail's music box. Or that her saying "I have to stay here" maybe had nothing to do with a social studies assignment.

Instead, I did something I never do. I shut up.

But the idea stuck in my mind. Maybe that

was Abigail Purser. And maybe she was telling me thanks for the hunk of Berlin Wall. And maybe, just maybe, she saw a little bit of herself in me. Toni said that the Day of the Dead was for welcoming spirits back to earth. Maybe that was really her ghost. Maybe.

As Gary trudged on, I turned back and murmured, "'Bye, Abigail."

There was no answer. No girl in a yellow dress.

But as I ran to catch up with Gary, I heard a girl's laughter behind me.

"Did you hear that?" I asked Gary. Now I was sure that girl was the ghost of Abigail Williams.

My Word
by Linda Ellerbee

MY NAME IS LINDA ELLERBEE. You may have noticed by now that Casey and I are somewhat alike. For one thing, we both like finding out other people's secrets. For another, we both hate it when other people find out our secrets.

For instance, my father was a wonderful man and I love him very much. Except when he drank. Because of that, I would sometimes be afraid to invite friends over to spend the night. What if my father came home drunk? I couldn't stand it if that happened. Also, my mother told me never to mention my father's drinking to anyone. We must, she told me, keep it a secret. That made the situation seem even worse to me than it was. I thought there was something very shameful about my family.

But, you see, we didn't know back then that alcoholism was a disease. (We thought it was weakness on my father's part.) We didn't know how common his disease was. We didn't know there were treatments. We didn't know how to help him, or how to help him find help. Or how to help ourselves. We just worried what everybody would think if they knew about Daddy. And so we lied. All of us. And I lived with the shame of my lying, too.

Later someone smart told me that we are only as sick as our secrets. It was an important lesson for me.

Today I understand that none of us is perfect. We sometimes disappoint others. We sometimes disappoint ourselves. We are not always the people we mean to be. But that doesn't mean we have to live with shame. And we all have secrets. But that doesn't mean we have to lie. What we do "have to" do is learn more about who we are, what we are, and that *we are all more alike than we are different*. It's only that our differences are easier to define.

But those differences can be wonderful. My father, although he had a disease called alcoholism, also taught me to love books, to hit a baseball, to ride a horse, to dream big—and to believe in the essential goodness of most humans.

It is a gray world we live in. People do not fit neatly into boxes. Neither do answers.

Casey learns this lesson in this book. So does Toni. So does Gary.

Me, I'm still working on learning. But then, I'm not as smart as Casey, Toni, or Gary. Or you.

Can you accept yourself for who you are and others for who they are? Of course you can. You're not dumber than grown-ups, just shorter. So get to it.

Get real.